People of the Bayou

People

of the Bayou

Christopher Hallowell

Cajun Life in
Lost America

drawings by Joe Deffes

E. P. Dutton   New York

For information contact:
E. P. Dutton, 2 Park Avenue, New York, N.Y. 10016

Library of Congress Cataloging in Publication Data
Hallowell, Christopher
People of the bayou.

1. Louisiana—Social life and customs. 2. Cajuns. 3. Country life—Louisiana. 4. Louisiana—Rural conditions. 5. Hallowell, Christopher, L. I. Title.
F376.H34   1979   976.3'06   79-12904

ISBN: 0-525-17728-0

Published simultaneously in Canada by Clarke, Irwin & Company Limited, Toronto and Vancouver

Designed by Mary Beth Bosco
10 9 8 7 6 5 4 3 2 1
First Edition

For those who love the marsh

Contents

Acknowledgments

Without the generosity and friendship of the people mentioned in these pages, I could not have written this book. They took the time to open the marsh and their love of it to me. There are others who also gave their time and showed their patience. First, I want to thank Willa Zakin for her enthusiasm, ideas, and companionship during much of my travel in south Louisiana. I am especially grateful to Greg Linscombe of the Louisiana Wildlife and Fisheries Commission and Gerald Voisin of the Louisiana Land and Exploration Company. Among the many people who also provided invaluable information, I want to mention the following: Sherwood Gagliano, Ned Simmons, Allan Ensminger, W. Guthrie Perry, Jr., Charley Hutchens, Ross Vincent, Eugene Turner, Russell "Doc" Brownell, and Warren, Johnny, and Daniel Price. Many other people volunteered information—too many for me to name. I am grateful to them all.

Preface

There are not many places in the United States where people still live off the land. But in parts of south Louisiana this is common. Thousands of people at the edge of the marshland that skirts the Gulf of Mexico spend their lives trapping animals for fur, dredging oysters, trawling for shrimps, or pursuing other forms of marine and marsh life that thrive in this fertile and wet region. They do not lead a hand-to-mouth existence. They sell their daily harvests for cash. In this way they have moved closer to the mainstream of American economic life, but with one foot resting on deeply planted traditions quite foreign to the lives most of us lead. This book is about these people and the environment they live in, one that never ceases influencing their lives.

People have heard about south Louisiana. It's different. Its food is spicy and rich; the descendants of Evangeline—the Cajuns—live there; and lazy bayous wind along levees where sagging old live oaks grow next to antebellum mansions. Life is slow. But this is only the surface of south Louisiana, one that doesn't show anything about the length and complexity of human history in this part of the state. Roots here go down deeper than in most regions of the country. The sprawling marsh, built by the Mississippi River, is even less well known. Yet it makes up much of south Louisiana. Only trappers and those others who actually live in it can appreciate its attraction. Visitors—hunters, sportsfishermen, and oil-drilling work crews—go into it to take from it. Trappers do this too, but they also like just to be there, in the lonely heart of the region.

That was a discovery I made after I got to know some trappers. When I saw the marsh for the first time a few years ago, it was from a plane. I was on a flight from New York to New Orleans that arrived in midafternoon of a sparkling December day. As the plane neared its destination, it swung south over the brown waters at the mouth of the Mississippi and then flew low right up the delta. The marsh was just under me. The air was so clear that I felt as though I could reach out and touch the grass. Bayous wove about, quiet and glistening, their brown-green waters broken from time to time by long strings of snow geese that looked like the crests of waves. Little houses on stilts dotted the levees. Most of them were separated from one another by miles and miles of marsh. It was a lost piece of America about to sink into the Gulf. I wanted to find out who lived in the houses and what it was like to have thousands of acres of grass, ponds, bayous, and islands in your backyard, with not a person to be seen.

In the loneliness of this region, people are shy. They eye strangers warily. Transportation, restricted to boat, is difficult and uncertain. One can spend days wandering the bayous trying to reach a point only a few miles away. A number of people helped me find my way, either by pointing the direction or by taking me where I wanted to go. I hope I have thanked them enough.

As the marsh breeds wariness, it also encourages kindness. Marsh dwellers look out for each other. No one can afford to be without friends in such vastness. That is one reason families are so big. After the initial shyness wears away, generosity shines through—the most genuine and uninhibited I have ever seen. It is a rare gift today and one I will always remember with gratitude.

C. H.

People of the Bayou

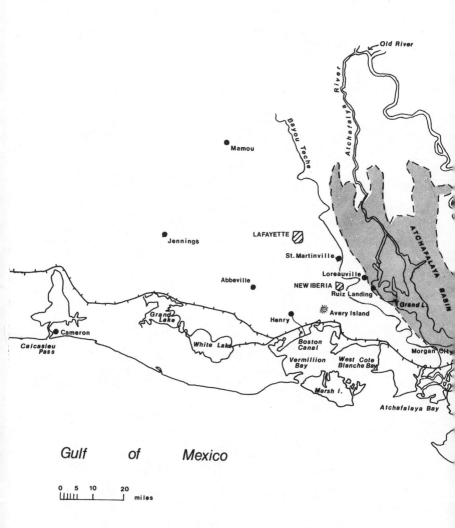

Old River

Atchafalaya River

Bayou Teche

Mamou

LAFAYETTE

St. Martinville

Jennings

Loreauville

ATCHAFALAYA BASIN

Abbeville

NEW IBERIA

Ruiz Landing

Grand L.

Grand Lake

Henry

Avery Island

Cameron

Calcasieu Pass

White Lake

Boston Canal

Morgan City

Vermillion Bay

West Cote Blanche Bay

Marsh I.

Atchafalaya Bay

Gulf of Mexico

0 5 10   20 miles

SOUTH LOUISIANA

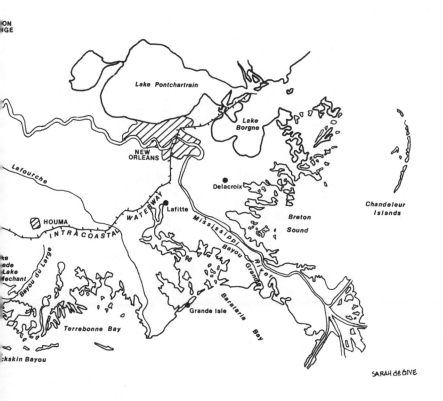

ON
GE

Lake Pontchartrain

Lake
Borgne

Lafourche

NEW
ORLEANS

Delacroix

Chandeleur
Islands

WATERWAY

Lafitte

Mississippi

Breton

Sound

HOUMA

INTRACOASTAL

Bayou

ke
ade
Lake
echant

Bayou du Large

Grande

River

Barataria

Bay

Grande Isle

Terrebonne Bay

kskin Bayou

SARAH deGIVE

One

Marsh Family

The little shed and wharf hanging over the water were just visible halfway down the canal. At the sound of the boat, Clifford Stelly came onto the wharf to watch its approach. In one hand he held a bedraggled pelt, which he began lashing back and forth with a rhythmic motion, so that droplets of water showed as a fine mist about his short white brush of hair. Now he tossed the skin into a bucket that overflowed with others like it. As he stood waiting, he rested one hand on his waist and the other against his thigh, tilting over ever so slightly, one arm supporting his barrel-like torso. His hands were the most massive I had ever seen.

After I had climbed onto the planks with my knapsack, Clifford offered me one of these hands and glanced at me shyly. But then, shifting his eyes away to the muddy water of the canal, he withdrew the hand before I had a chance to extend my own. "I think my hand's too dirty to shake; I been workin' with them rats." He made a sweeping gesture toward them.

Animal corpses were everywhere in various attitudes of death—on the benches, on the floor, along the wharf, and in the boats tied to the wharf. There were more nutrias among them than muskrats. The nutrias' huge incisors were a shining orange, and their ratlike tails splayed out from the piled-up skins like seaweed from rocks. A heap of skinned and gutted carcasses lay bunched up near one door of the shed, their gunmetal-blue entrails in a plastic tub next to them, while the pelts soaked in a washbasin near by. More pelts hung on racks outside, swinging to and fro as they dried in the chilly wind, the sun glinting off the guard hairs.

Three of Clifford's five sons—Randall, Wyndal, and Blaine—were also in the shed. Standing before a bench, each had a knife in his hand and a nutria lying in front of him. Their sidelong glances at me were timid but ill-concealed. Beyond the most meager greeting, they scarcely said a word. Their work hid their shyness. Randall made quick cuts around the paws of a nutria. The movements of his knife were no more traceable than flashes of light. His visored cap was awry and his cigar stub was awash with saliva. After making the four cuts, he sliced between the back paws and the base of the tail, shoving his hand underneath the skin of the animal's back to separate it from the flesh. With the pelt suddenly loosened from its body, the nutria appeared to be draped in a luxurious fur coat. Randall picked up the animal and heaved it across the shed. It landed on the bench near Wyndal or Blaine with the heavy thud of a bag of laundry.

Every so often one of the brothers murmured something in French and received a guttural reply, also in French, sometimes followed by a belly laugh. This was particularly noticeable in Randall, whose ample stomach bounced up and down. This was Cajun French, some of whose clipped staccato phrasing dates back to seventeenth-century usage. Verb endings sounded different from those of contemporary French. The pronouns would confound the teachings of any French grammar book. It was only the frequent interspersal of English words that permitted me to follow the movement of the talk.

Blaine, a round-faced nineteen-year-old with a penchant for sudden observations, was talking about catfish. "Mo pense qu'il fait trop cold pour les catfish."

"Mais non, man," retorted Randall, "m'en ai attrapé hier. Good ones." He threw his cigar stub into the canal. "Plus grand que ça, anyway." His belly shook with laughter.

"M'espère, 'cause if they was smaller, serait difficil skin, non."

Amid the bantering, the second stage of the skinning fell to Wyndal and to Blaine, who stood side by side at another bench. Wyndal plunked each animal down on its hindlegs so that it sat upright and, for one split second, had the winsome look of a pet. Then, with movements too fast to follow, his hand shoved the head down between the shoulders so that the back arched. The skin seemed to fly up and over the contorted body. He whirled the half-naked body around, flung its hindfeet into an iron chock, and pulled the skin over the head. Then he cut the skin away from the skull—gently around the eyes, nose, and mouth—pulled it free, gave it a shake, and tossed it into the washbasin, later to be stretched and dried.

The denuded corpses ended up on the floor. Mink ranchers from Michigan and Wisconsin would buy them as food for their animals. But they could be sold only after being gutted and having their paws and teeth cut away. This task fell to Charlyne, one of the three Stelly daughters. She spent every morning on the cold wharf, stoically cutting and chopping with a hatchet and dumping the entrails and appendages into the canal.

I commented to Wyndal about the pace of the work. He looked up at me with a shy smile. "Yeah, you jus' git used to it; that's all. I been doin' this ma whole life."

The three brothers can skin fifty nutrias in half an hour, but this is not really fast work. The little town of Cameron, perched on the edge of the Gulf, holds an annual fur festival that brings trappers from miles around. Side by side with a beauty contest is the muskrat- and nutria-skinning contest. The winners each year will be able to skin three muskrats in well under a minute and a nutria in about half a minute. Their reputations spread all through the marsh. But this kind of speed is short-lived. Trapping as a serious business requires some pacing, and anyway, trappers are rarely in a hurry.

The Stellys' cabin is connected to the shed by a boardwalk on stilts. The cabin stands perched on the levee above Boston Canal; behind it stretches the vast Louisiana marsh. Three children's swings that hang from a metal frame just to the left of the cabin are the only geometrical arrangement about the place; everything else is simply an accumulation. An old gas stove sits in the grass near a corner of the cabin, with a rusted frying pan on one burner. Derelict electricity generators occupy the muddy grass in back of the cabin. "We uses six every year," Clifford tells me, with a note of pride. "We works 'em real hard out here." Oil drums are also scattered about. Narrow aluminum boats, some partially filled with water, line a little canal at the edge of the marsh behind the cabin. One adornment particularly strikes me—a table whose frame was once the dashboard structure of a car. The ancient steering wheel, speedometer, and throttle are still in place. The children who are forever scampering about compete for the honor of traveling to imaginary places in this strange vehicle. But their imaginations can carry them no further than a few miles out into the marsh or up Boston Canal; that is all they know. The remains of steel traps are everywhere—rusting jaws, broken springs, chains, and pans litter the ground under the cabin so thickly that the hut appears built on a heap of traps.

The cabin itself is orderly enough to give some relief from the clutter around it, though one would guess that construction came to a halt just as soon as the roof and the four walls were secure. Strips of tar paper shield the back and sides from damp winter winds. Sheets of plywood painted gray give the front the look of an army barracks. But this is an impression that quickly ends upon entering the dwelling. It is dark and perpetually cool inside, the light from the small windows reflecting dully off the bare linoleum underfoot. Battered furniture crowds against the simulated wood paneling of the living room/kitchen. The number of chairs and scattered bits of personal property lying about—cigarette packs, shoes, hats, and jackets—bear witness to a sizable congregation here, fully occupying the darkened bedrooms whose doors stand ajar. Decorations are few, a sign that the camp is a place of work rather than leisure. A couple of paintings of wildlife by a sixteen-year-old daughter, Dena, show an untrained hand but an eye sensitive to color. The only other noticeable adornments are a gleaming, stylized representation of ducks in flight on one of the walls, deer antlers that serve as a hat rack, and over a sofa a plate on which is inscribed: "When I works, I works hard. When I sits, I sits loose. When I thinks, I falls asleep."

The family spends every autumn and most of each winter here, far out in the marsh. In coming here, Clifford and his sons follow a tradition established generations ago. In November, when the summer's heat and humidity give way to cooler winds, thousands of Louisiana fur trappers head for the marsh with their families, leaving their inland homes and jobs until the following spring. The migration is so deeply instilled that many people in south Louisiana regard it as instinctive. Clifford jokes about it in his quiet way. "Ah don' know why ah likes it out here. Trappin's a terrible business. Lookit all the blood an' mess. All the money's gone out of it. But if ah could, ah'd stay right here all year 'round, where ah don' have no one to bother me an' ah got all the food ah needs right here at ma feets."

Even though few trappers articulate the reasons why they do it, this occupation is the common denominator of Louisiana marsh life. Those who follow it seem to mimic the movements of hundreds of thousands of migratory birds that flock to the marsh and leave it on an annual cycle. In the spring, trappers scatter once again. Some, like Clifford, go back to their fields of rice or sugarcane. Others return to jobs with some branch of the omnipresent petroleum and natural gas industry. Wyndal and Randall are among these people. Wyndal is a welder who puts together the behemoth-sized oil-well platforms that are now fixtures of the Gulf. Randall is a foreman in a pipe yard, but says he doesn't do anything but "sit aroun' until they need some pipe an' then work for a couple of hours an' then sit aroun' again until ah goes crazy gittin' bored."

Older trappers go back to occupations that let them harvest the nearby resources. A man who traps a freshwater marsh may merely change equipment and lay some hoop nets in the bayou for catfish, or he may turn to crawfishing. Some who trap near the edge of the Gulf will dredge for oysters or trawl for shrimps. Others do nothing except odd jobs. There is really no need to do anymore, since the marsh provides them a living. A chicken neck tied to a string will fill a bucket with crabs in half an hour. Catfish bite on almost anything. Oysters line the banks of many bayous. Rabbits thrive on the levees, and sometimes the marsh is overrun with ducks and geese.

The Stellys, particularly the sons, could certainly make more money if they didn't trap. The hours are long and the returns can be meager. But most other occupations would not allow them to stay in the marsh for weeks at a time. The family greets each dawn in a state of low-keyed excitement tempered by skepticism concerning the weather, whose mood can change with remarkable speed during the winter. Clifford and his three sons mill about the cabin in their stocking feet. They down cup after cup of coffee and mumble comments about the weather, the coming day's trapping, their planned whereabouts, and their expectations. Clifford's wife, Della, stands quietly at the stove, frying huge portions of bacon and eggs. A dull light filters through the frost-clouded window above the stove and onto her frizzy gray hair. The tilt of her head betrays a careful attention to what is being said. Occasionally she turns around and in a singsong voice asks a question that clearly reveals her anxiety about the departure of her husband and sons into the marsh.

The talk is slow, a step or two behind the brightening sky. "I bet them nutr'a ran some las' night. It sure was cold 'nough for 'em," says Wyndal.

"It's gonna be cold 'nough for me out there this mornin'," observes Blaine. "Hey, didya hear that Virgil got his fingers fros'bit yesti'dy mornin'? That's what I heared on the radio."

"Me, ah think maybe the marsh be iced over this mornin'. She dropped down to twenty-five las' night," Clifford adds. "There's gonna be ice out there unless the sun come out good. A couple of more days of this an' the ice gonna freeze up them nutr'as' tails." He sidles up a little closer to the cabin's single gas heater and says with a sheepish grin, "Ah goin' wait a little bit 'fore ah goes out."

Clifford's leadership of the family is so detached and unostentatious as to be almost automatic. His wife, children, and grandchildren look to him for direction, and he provides it with a murmur or a gentle wave of the hand. He may say, while he warms himself at the stove, "Blaine, check the trotline later an' see if we got us any catfish, huh." Blaine barely acknowledges the request. But it is sure to be obeyed.

The meandering conversation subsides entirely with the appearance of the bacon and eggs, which are consumed in a matter of minutes. It is as though the food signaled the real beginning of the day, bringing a certain tension into the cabin. Randall wipes his mouth with his sleeve and tugs on his boots. Blaine bustles about collecting a variety of gear—additional traps, a .22 rifle, life jackets, and a torn slicker. He invites me to go with him.

An artificial channel—*trainasse* in local French parlance—leads from the rear of the cabin to Lake Hébert, about a mile across the marsh. Blaine dumps his gear into the ice-coated bottom of an outboard at the head of the channel. He is about to jump in, but suddenly he pauses. "Almost forgot to feed Newt," he says, running over to a cage near the shed where skins are stretched and dried. In the cage, an almost full grown nutria is already moving its incisors up and down in anticipation of the carrots and lettuce Blaine is about to bring. But before he feeds it, Blaine takes the animal out of the cage, holds it in his arms, and caresses its thick fur.

"I catched his mammy in a trap last year. I didn't knowed she had little ones, but the nex' day I come by an' seed two little babies settin' on a clump of grass. I brought 'em both back, but one died. But Newt here, he good an' strong. I think he's gonna have babies, but it's hard to tell with these animals. The males and the females, they looks jus' about the same."

His hand travels up and down the nutria's back, around the neck behind the ears, and down the back again in a single steady movement. The nutria shifts its beady eyes ceaselessly. Its long whiskers gyrate back and forth, set in motion by the movement of the incisors, and its tail hangs limply toward the ground.

"He don' like children though. He'll try to take a bite right outta their fingers. At times I let him outta the cage at night an' he goes into the marsh. But in the mornin', he's settin' right in front of his cage waitin' for a carrot."

After giving the animal a last scratch on the head, Blaine puts the animal back into the cage and throws in a couple of carrots. We watch for a moment as Newt sniffs them and then begins nibbling on one with quick bites. Then Blaine trots back to the boat and we start off down the channel. The marsh grass flashes by, ducks lift from potholes, and fish swirl out of our path. The channel is no more than five feet wide, leaving about six inches of water on either side of the boat. Narrow passages such as this crisscross the marsh. Most of them were made long ago by trappers who wanted easy access to its interior. The older ones were hewn out by hand. In the 1920s, marsh buggies came along—treaded monsters with bargelike bodies that hauled great plows behind them and heaved the muck to one side. Now, most such channels are dredged out with draglines that gobble up all the ooze and vegetation in a straight line and dump it beside the channel. The Stellys' ditch was made that way. It runs straight and true, five feet wide and three feet deep in high water, like a part down the middle of a scalp. When Blaine is not trapping, he operates a commercial dragline. But he rarely talks about this; it's just a way to earn money.

The traps are set along the edge of the ditch and around the shore of Lake Hébert—one hundred sixty of them—a line of deadly steel jaws ready to snap closed on the legs of animals. A tall pole topped by a strip of white cloth marks each trap. The poles also serve to anchor the traps. As we come up to some of them, white flags thrashing back and forth show that an animal is struggling to free itself.

Blaine seems oblivious to the jerking flags. I guess that he is going to the end of the trapline on the other side of the lake and will then work his way back. The first trap at the end of the line holds a big nutria. A mature animal weighs about sixteen pounds, solidly built with about the proportions of a beaver or a groundhog. Its broad rear paws are webbed except between the fourth and fifth toes, making it possible for the animal to get a grip on slippery mud banks and to clutch blades of grass. The head is square and solid looking. The nose is firmly planted, the forehead wide, and the teeth so prominent as to draw all one's attention.

As we approach the first nutria on foot, the gnashing of those teeth makes even the shrill cry of killdeer rising from the mudflats inaudible. The animal is caught high up on the right rear leg. Coated in mud, it has worn a circle around the pole during the long night of thrashing about, with no chance of escape. Now it paces back and forth around the perimeter of the circle on the far side of the pole. It gives a series of mighty tugs in an effort to wrench its body away, grinding its teeth all the while.

When we are almost on top of it, the animal lunges. Blaine leaps aside shouting, "You git too close to them teeth, an he'll take yer leg off."

Trappers club their captured animals to death. It's not a nice sight. Perhaps nutrias are fortunate that their skulls are so thin, despite a massive appearance. At any rate, they die quickly. Otters and raccoons have tough skulls that sometimes require five or six blows to crack. A nutria's head will split under just one.

Blaine holds out the end of his club, the "killing stick" as he calls it, and the nutria goes for that. "I always do this. If you git' em with their heads out, you got a good target. But when they's all huddled up an' snarlin' at you, an' you hit 'em, you can miss the heads an' hurt the fur."

The nutria strikes at the end of the club and Blaine raises the stick behind his shoulder, leaving the animal still straining, neck extended, and almost motionless with eyes bulging. In the next split second, it is thrashing on the ground, blood spurting from the top of its head and nostrils and soaking into the dark mud, legs thrusting out crazily in all directions. Blaine brings the club down again and takes the limp body out of the trap. The skin and muscle on the leg near where the jaws snapped have been scoured through to the bone.

Louisiana fur trappers, not unexpectedly, are the targets of sporadic campaigns to ban the use of leg-hold traps. Most of them just shrug the matter off. "If those peoples ever came out here and saw all them nutr'a, they'd think different," Clifford told me. But the Louisiana Wildlife and Fisheries Commission takes the protests more to heart than do the trappers. In 1976, staff biologists introduced some trappers to a type of trap designed to kill an animal almost instantly by crushing it. The trappers didn't like these traps one bit. "They

broke on us all the time," Clifford says, "an' they was too big to put in the nutr'a runways. We weren't catchin' nothin' in them." The same consensus coursed through the marsh, arming the commission with pro-leg-hold lobbying ammunition if the animal welfare people ever really press the issue: they can say, correctly, that the new traps will put trappers out of business.

Even so, a bill to prohibit leg-hold traps would make little headway in the state legislature if examples of past attitudes toward animals suggest anything. Some years ago, efforts were afoot to ban cockfighting, and a bill to that effect was introduced. By thirty-one to seven, the state senate voted that chickens were not animals; the senators never saw fit to reclassify chickens, but the point was brought home that participation in cockfighting was the inalienable right of every Louisianan.

Blaine found forty-odd nutrias in his traps that morning. A few of them were young ones that he let go. They hobbled away to shelter in clumps of marsh grass. He also got half a dozen muskrats. They were all dead, the victims at some time during the night of either trauma or drowning. Some of the traps were sprung but quite empty, others empty except for the claws of nutrias or muskrats. When we came to a sprung trap, the look on Blaine's open face changed to one of bewilderment, as though encountering an undeserved slight. He always moved carefully around the area, searching the grass and mud for some clue to how the animal had escaped. During these searches, he muttered to himself in a tone of chastisement before resetting the trap. But when he came on a trap that held a nutria or a muskrat, he rarely expressed pleasure at his own success, only at the beauty of the fur. "Lookit the pelt on that animal," he would observe. "That'll make someone a purty coat. I don' know how they make those. It must take a lot of animals. They must cost somethin' though, huh?"

As we headed back to the cabin, Blaine suddenly began shouting above the roar of the outboard. "Ya know, I only went up to the seventh grade. When I tol' my daddy I was quittin' school, he was mad. Maybe I shoulda stayed, but if I had I wouldn't be comin' out here. I'd probably have a different job somewheres an' they wouldn't let me take the trappin' season off. I sure couldn't take that."

As the men return with their catches during the day and dump them in the small shed, the conversation takes on an edge of rivalry. Victors or losers, they hang over the benches, spit into the canal, and smoke their cigarettes.

"Man, was it cold out there this mornin'," says Randall, pushing his forever drooping eyeglasses up on the bridge of his nose.

"Well, you shoulda waited like ah done." Clifford hoists his body upright from its customary tilted position. The change in posture forewarns of humor. "When ah got out there, ah thought ah was 'bout to die from heat stroke."

"Sure, jus' like one of them what you call 'em, polar bears up nor'. If I been with you, I coulda cooled you off with a bucket of water. Yessir, what's that temperature say now? Forty-five degrees. That's hot." Pleased with this response, Randall pulls his sagging pants up on his rounded stomach and struts around the shed in a little circle.

"Well, we sure got us some animals las' night, though. They was runnin' good," Wyndal says, breaking a few minutes of silence.

"Yeah, an' ah almost got an' otter, me," Clifford says with a note of regret. "Ah seen his tracks all roun' one of my sets. But he didn't go in. They's too smart. You gotta be settin' for 'em if you want to catch any."

Conversations start up and trail off into silence. Soon someone takes out a knife and picks up a nutria. Clifford begins skinning the muskrats. Older trappers prefer to work with muskrats, leaving the nutrias to their sons. A muskrat requires less work to skin but more expertise in cutting, for its skin is delicate. People like Clifford grew up skinning muskrats. He scarcely looks at the animal while he does it.

As the skinning continues, Della and the wives of the three sons come out of the cabin and watch the men, or perhaps wash some of the skins and hang them up to dry in the sun. Children are forever in and out of the shed and are always being watched over by the adults. Della assumes the role of supervisor over the children and the other women as well as the guardian of the men. The set of her wide blue eyes in a round, soft face gives her a gentle, caring look.

Just as Clifford directs the family in its use of the marsh, Della reigns over the kitchen. It is her pride to lay a good table; the more food on it, the better. She spends most of the hours of the day in the kitchen, either cutting or stirring. One afternoon when she was hovering over a pot of gumbo, she turned to me and handed me a spoon. "Here, you tastes that and tells me what you think. We're going to add some crabs later on, but we don't have 'em yet. So you jus' take a taste the way it is now. Go ahead."

I dipped into the thick stew, in which floated bits of a bell pepper, onion, okra, and shrimp, and took a taste.

"It's good, non?" She lowered her voice and confided, in a voice barely containing its pride, "We eats good here. Mais yeah, cher. No one goes hungry here."

Della cherishes being able to feed her family well, just as Clifford cherishes the marsh. The combination is fortunate, for much of the food she cooks comes from the marsh and is gathered by Clifford and his sons. Food gathering is the usual afternoon activity. Blaine goes out to Lake Hébert to check and bait the catfish trotline. Wyndal pulls in the crab traps and gingerly removes a dozen big blue claws for the gumbo. Randall wrestles some garfish from the gill net's mesh, their slack gaping jaws lined with needlelike teeth. During the shrimping season, Clifford trawls in Vermilion Bay.

The results of the afternoon's harvest bring the men together in the shed, usually to clean fish. Each catfish is strung up on a hook and its skin is pulled off with pincers, usually while it is still alive. The bloody thing flaps grotesquely from the hook until someone takes it down and hammers it to death. The garfish are laid out on the benches and skinned in more delicate fashion.

Della or one of her daughters-in-law comes out with a washbasin to collect the ingredients for the evening meal. The men remain in the dying light of the shed for a while longer, talking in gentler tones and comparing notes on the day's activities. At this time of day, a stillness settles over the marsh. The boarded-up summer cabins along Boston Canal blend into the deepening colors of the marsh. The grasses stop waving, and the canal is now so calm that the water has an icelike sheen all the way to Vermilion Bay. Reluctantly, the men begin to gravitate toward the cabin. They may pause for a moment to sit on the doorstep, using the excuse of taking off their boots to linger outside a moment longer.

This is the time of day when they seem content to just sit. Inside, they tilt back in their chairs and listlessly watch the television screen, keeping an ear always cocked toward the CB radio, which likewise stays on from before daybreak until well into the night. No one pays much overt attention to either TV or radio, but neither is totally ignored. Both offer instant companionship. When gossip and shop talk run thin, all eyes turn to the television until a distraction of another sort draws their combined attention. It might be the voice of a friend on the CB radio, full of French and static and the boastful talk of shrimpers returning from the Gulf. Occasionally a call comes in for a member of the family. For each one of them, there is an identifying CB name, given by a friend or relative, that amounts to a crystallized image of the person. Clifford's CB name is Big Parain, and Della's is Big Nanan—Cajun French for godfather and godmother, respectively. Randall is the Muskrat; Wyndal is the Forked Island Welder.

Children are another distraction. They are the family clowns, and they constitute the glue that binds families together. With their actions constantly followed, they learn early how charm earns lavish displays of affection. Toby James, Randall's toddling son, is usually the star of the pre-dinner family gathering. As a result of an ear infection that left him deaf for a time, he is a strangely quiet child, absorbed in a private world. Before an operation that cured his deafness, the family communicated to him by signs; even now they still gesticulate to attract his attention. Frequently, when the CB radio is quiet, conversation momentarily exhausted, and when eyes have not yet turned to the television, Toby James steps forth on little legs so plump they do not quite straighten. Instantly becoming the center of attention, he stares at the circle of faces as half a dozen or more hands rise in the air in greeting. "Hi ya, Toby James; hi ya," echoes through the cabin. The child looks up uncertainly at the faces. Clifford pads over to him with an outstretched hand. "Gimme five, Toby James," he says, "gimme five." Toby James stares into Clifford's grizzled face, blinks, and tentatively lifts his tiny hand as Clifford's huge one gently encircles it.

The distractions that unite the family at this time of day are climaxed by the meal. But if it is the evening's main event, it is also the quietest one. Della and the other women pile the little kitchen table high with gumbo, rice, boiled vegetables, fried catfish, and garfish balls, as well as a selection of homemade jams and hot sauces and the inevitable loaf of Evangeline Maid—white bread so soft that it hangs limply over the table's edge. Once the plates are filled, members of the family scatter to the chairs around the living area. They are silent, hunching over to gobble down the food.

In the tiredness that now prevails, the allure of the television screen is strong, even though no one is entirely seduced by it. This is also a time for affection. Wyndal's children crawl onto his lap and he swings them in the air. Husbands and wives sit side by side on a couch, talking in low tones. They smile at each other; some hold hands or rest a palm on the other's thigh in a somewhat awkward closeness.

The interlude does not last long. One by one the men drift out through the door, followed by the older children, toward the warmth of the stretching and drying shack. Here the next few hours will be spent tacking nutria skins to wooden molds and slipping muskrat skins over wire stretchers. The end of the day, the big meal, the close heat from the two kerosene stoves in the shed prompt a mood of joviality, a babble accompanied by the ceaseless tap-tap of the hammers as they work.

Dena, sidling up to Randall and Wyndal, says playfully, "You hit them nails like that an' you goin' to pound yer thumb."

"That's what you said las' night an' it didn't happen, did it?" Wyndal retorts with his shy smile.

"That's what she done said las' night and the night afore that an'

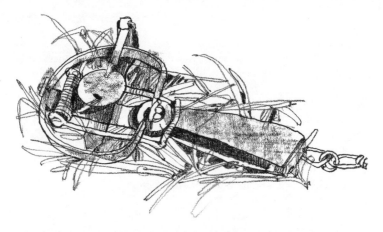

the one afore that," Randall declares with a chuckle. "Her voice box starts repeatin' itself at this time a night, I guess."

Dena giggles, "That's jus' what you says to me every night, so I guess it's yer voice box that's broke."

Clifford is in the next room with Shelly, his youngest son, who is fourteen years old. They are taking dried skins off the molds and arranging them in a stack. They both listen to the conversation and smile. Each time another skin is added, everyone looks at it. At the end of the evening, when the stack is waist-high, the family in the shed stands back to admire it. Blaine stretches his arm out at eye level and says, "If them nutr'a are runnin' tonight, she be up to here tomorrow."

No one says anything in particular, but there are nods as one by one they go back to the cabin. The women and most of the children have long since gone to bed. Before he comes in, Clifford turns the generator off. The silence of the marsh pervades the cabin as the generator's last chug and sputter die away.

Two

A Delta's Life

Boston Canal, where the Stellys' cabin is located, begins in the tiny agricultural community of Henry, set in the middle of cow pastures and rice fields. Three minutes along the canal into the marsh from the community, the only hint of human activity is the throb of tugs on the Intracoastal Canal and the sight of an oil derrick in the distance. Strings of snow geese crisscross the canal, and egrets lift themselves in stately attitudes. Even during the dreariest winter days, the marsh is alive with birds. Ducks and geese winter here by the hundreds of thousands. Shorebirds—dowitchers, snipe, plover, stilt, and yellowlegs, to name but a few—flit at the edges of the waterways to dabble in the endless feast along the banks. Herons station themselves in the shallows in poses of unmoving concentration.

This is a bewildering land, wild and lonely in its isolation but also tamed by the prevalence of canals dug by the petroleum industry. Across the soggy reaches, the canals form a maze of right angles and dead-end channels. But in the silence, the alien shapes of oil and gas wells with their silver-painted valves, gauges, nuts, and pipes are strangely unobtrusive, as though all this technological gadgetry had been abandoned and forgotten. The canals appear similarly deserted, as though man, once his digging was done, had been content to leave the marsh to itself.

A trapper may walk the marsh all day long or nose a boat through its endless bayous, channels, and *creveys*—the Cajun word for its water-filled ponds and lagoons—and never see another person. The

expanse of waving grass can swallow a man in no time. Not many roads have been built across this land; there is nothing for a road to be built on. Such solid thoroughfares as there are usually follow the high ground of the levees alongside the bayous. They may be no more than eight or ten feet wide and only a few feet above the surrounding marsh. Still other roads follow the northern edge of the marsh, sometimes dipping into it for a short distance. Everywhere, the flatness of the landscape, with its fields of sugarcane and rice, is broken only by lines of towering live oaks draped with Spanish moss, an occasional tumbledown house, or a tiny settlement with one general store beside an intersection. The roads careen across this flatness, seeming never to lead anywhere except to other roads that lead to yet others, so that one's destination becomes elusive. The intersections have disconcerting similarity. I have often approached one with the feeling that half an hour ago or two hours ago—or it may have been last week—I was approaching the same intersection, with the same sagging barn and the same live oak beside a sugarcane field. Yet, in the midst of a landscape suspended in time, one can always somehow sense the direction of the marsh. Perhaps it is the ever so slight downward tilt of the land, or the lazy flow of the bayous, that gives it away.

In all, Louisiana has four and one-half million acres of marsh spreading across the southern edge of the state for a width of about three hundred miles, rather like a frayed picnic blanket beside a vast lake. Woven into its fabric are over one hundred plant species, bearing such curious names as sensitive jointvetch, rattlebox, floating-heart, and stinking fleabane. The most prevalent species is wiregrass, whose clumps provide a soft appearance. The presence of the marsh is obvious ten minutes outside New Orleans. From the ragged edge of the Gulf of Mexico, it extends inland in some places for five miles, in others for almost one hundred miles, gradually changing, the further inland it goes, from saline to brackish to fresh water. In a few places the marsh never really ends, but shifts by degrees into swamp, where cypress and tupelo gums and crayfish abound. The most notable of these places is the Atchafalaya Swamp, the biggest swamp in the country and one of the few remaining that depends on the annual cycle of flooding and drying out.

The Mississippi River created the marsh, and in a few places it is still doing so—flooding, depositing its sediment, and all the while, as though with one single-minded purpose, emptying its waters into the Gulf with as little struggle as possible. The sediment carried by the river is made up of some one million tons of sand, silt, and clay that are loosened each day from a watershed covering almost half the country's continental land mass and also the central Canadian provinces in a complicated filigree of waterways. This sediment is the foundation of the marsh. Concentrated in it is a rich blend of nutrients whose origins stretch from the crags of the Rockies to the hardwood forests that cover the western slope of the Adirondacks.

The process of building the marsh to its present size took only about seven thousand years—a mere blink of the eye as measured in geologic time. It took place flood by flood, layer by layer, delta by delta. Over the millennia, the Mississippi has laid down a number of deltas; their remains are the cornerstones of the south Louisiana landscape. Some geologists and geographers say there were five altogether; others say seven. The point is academic. Only one of these deltas still functions, but its lifeblood has all but ceased to flow through its veins as a result of man's manipulation. This delta's central artery, the Mississippi itself, has been so tampered with by the building of levees and other flood-control measures that its water can no longer probe into the marsh and build up the fragile land, now restricted to a long, narrow peninsula that reaches far out into the Gulf and ends in three prongs that resemble a bird's foot. In fact, "bird's-foot" is the name geographers give to a delta of this particular kind.

All the Mississippi's earlier deltas took on a more customary fan shape. Remnants of some of these are still quite evident. A little to the northeast of the present delta is a lovely necklace of islands called the Chandeleurs, most of which are included in the Breton Bird Refuge. Three thousand years ago, however, they constituted the seaward edge of a vast layer of sediment whose northern edge nuzzled close along the coastline of what is now the state of Mississippi. Most of this delta was submerged long ago. Chandeleur Sound now marks its resting place.

The remains of another big delta are now part of the Louisiana parishes of Terrebonne and Lafourche—a ragtag accumulation of islands, islets, channels, peninsulas, estuaries, and isthmuses just west of the Mississippi's present course. They are all that is left of a formation that dates back no more than a thousand years. Of the earliest identifiable delta laid down farther to the west between six and seven thousand years ago, no remains are visible. Part of it was covered by the Gulf's rising waters, and part was buried under later sediments.

Deltas live at the whim of the rivers that give them birth. All eventually wash away and are submerged. A river's natural tendency is always to reach its outlet by the easiest route possible. Similarly, it is the tendency of a newly created delta, as it expands, to grow increasingly complex: A sandbar springs up here, a channel branches off there, and everywhere mini-deltas are laid down. As this happens, the river's course grows longer and slower. At a certain point in the process, the lengthening route and lessening gradient begin to frustrate and impede the river's flow. Discovering a more direct passage becomes a matter of expediency. Sometimes one river takes over the course of another. The delta of the co-opting river then wastes away for lack of the building materials and nutrients that no longer reach it.

Since the 1940s, the Mississippi has been edging toward the course of the Atchafalaya River, the pulse of the swamp that bears its name. Beginning only one hundred forty miles north of the Gulf Coast and only five miles west of the Mississippi, the Atchafalaya flows more or less parallel to the latter; but its course is much straighter, not having developed all the coiling, serpentine meanders that characterize the lower Mississippi.

Nearly a century and a half ago, a man named Henry Shreve, who for years labored under the title of Superintendent of Western River

Improvement and for whom the industrialized Louisiana city of Shreveport is named, decided to cut a channel between the Atchafalaya and the Mississippi. Soon after, the Mississippi's current began to shift toward the new opening—which for some unknown reason came to be called Old River—and then to nibble away at the channel's freshly excavated banks. By the 1950s, Old River and the Atchafalaya were well on their way to forming the Mississippi's primary channel. The Army Corps of Engineers, reacting to the threat with a determination not even the Mississippi could subvert, proceeded to eliminate Old River by damming it up with dredged sand. A few miles upstream the corps created another channel across which it built a concrete and iron dam whose massive gates regulate the amount of water flowing through it to the Atchafalaya—from one-third of the Mississippi's total volume during periods of low water to as much as one-half when it is in flood.

Each year, enough sediment flows down the Atchafalaya to bury all of New York City under two hundred feet of ooze. One result of the engineers' hydraulic manipulation of the river's current has been the continuing destruction of the Atchafalaya Swamp—a development environmentalists have resisted for more than two decades in a series of battles with the corps. Another result has been the creation of yet another delta, this one in Atchafalaya Bay. The sight of the muddy water of the bay giving birth to land is an awesome one—a swirling and churning that gradually builds up a mudbar, which in its turn will blossom into a grass-covered marsh island. In Atchafalaya Bay the magical process is occurring with such rapidity that the two hundred square miles of the area may be entirely covered with marsh within twenty-five years. Already the alluvial form of the typical delta is taking shape, the only place along the Louisiana coast where the land mass is growing.

If Henry Shreve had not created Old River, the Mississippi probably would have remained innocent of the temptation to slide into the Atchafalaya's bed. And if the Corps of Engineers had not succeeded in its attempts to thwart that same seduction, the Mississippi by this time almost certainly would have adopted the course of the Atchafalaya, reducing its own present route to a mere trickle and leaving both New Orleans and Baton Rouge high and dry.

Not all the Louisiana marshes were created as a direct result of the delta-building process. While the Mississippi's mouth shifted back and forth along a two-hundred-mile section of low coastline, building and abandoning deltas, another geological process has been responsible for creating a marsh of a somewhat different character. Three forces have been at work here: the discharge of sediment into the Gulf by the Mississippi, the prevailing westward flow of the Gulf's own currents, and the erosion caused by waves and rain. The currents and erosion have consistently warred against one another. The victor in this war takes the sediment as its prize.

Just west of Vermilion Bay, where the Stellys trap nutrias and muskrats, the coastline is smooth—unruffled by estuaries, islands, or the maze of channels that are typical of the eastern half of the state. The marsh behind this gentle shore is likewise different. Its outlines are more regular, with less fraying at the edges. The only interruption in the flat blanket of waving grass is a series of low ridges running parallel to the shore, one behind the other, orderly as a marching regiment. Most of the ridges are lined with old and massive live oaks—some still growing, others transformed into silvery ghosts by the ravages of hurricanes. At an elevation of about ten feet, the dry, sandy soil of the ridges provides the trees a roothold that permits them to survive. For this reason, the Cajun French word, *chenière* (oak tree) has been applied to the elevations, which are also known as stranded beach ridges. They were, in fact, created by the constant war over sediment that produced the marsh. As the mouth of the Mississippi has shifted from east to west and back again, the marsh to the west has grown or receded. When the mouth of the river was farther to the west than it presently is, the westerly currents of the Gulf carried shoreward the silt, sand, and clay suspended in the water, so that the marsh crept out into the Gulf inch by inch; as the river mouth shifted farther to the east, gravity emptied the Gulf's currents of sediment, silt stopped building up, and the edges of the marsh began to crumble. The chenières were created as waves driven by southerly winds, along with torrential rains typical of south Louisiana, eroded the silt and clay, carrying them out to sea and piling the sand that remained into long ridges. Here young live oaks soon took root, clutching and binding the sand, until a soil firm enough to allow people to settle on it had been formed.

At the moment, with the Mississippi's mouth far to the east, the western marsh is receding. Inching upward is a beach ridge that will eventually form a barricade between the turmoil of the Gulf and the

smoothness of the marsh. This beach ridge will probably not last long. As sediment builds a delta in Atchafalaya Bay, lurking currents in the Gulf will begin carrying it to the west. Once again, silt will accumulate in the shallow waters adjacent to the beach ridge, and the process of marsh formation will continue.

It has always been the assumption in Louisiana that the tons of sediment dumped on its doorstep by the Mississippi must result in the physical growth of the state. This was true until a short time ago. But now the process has all but stopped. Except in Atchafalaya Bay, the marsh is progressively decaying.

In Louisiana, the Mississippi's annual floods used to provide the marsh with its nutrients. During the spring rampage, the river characteristically jumped its natural levees and dropped sand and silt in the shallow water. Plants took root there, giving the marsh its binding sinews. Now, the river can no longer deliver the nutrients.

Over the past century, man has changed the river. From Cairo, Illinois, to the Gulf, its natural levees have been reinforced, raised, and solidified in a flood-control program that as it subdued the churning currents has left the river trapped in its bed. Only in rare years of heavy precipitation, such as occurred in 1973, do the waters escape and inundate the marsh. In most years, the channelized course carries the river's sediment past the marsh and into the Gulf, where it sinks in the deep water. No longer able to receive its lifeblood, the marsh compacts and sinks. Eleven thousand acres have vanished into the Gulf each year during the last three decades.

As more and more of the marsh submerges, salt water creeps into the estuaries, killing off those plants that can live only in fresh or slightly saline water. A mere handful of the marsh's many plant species can tolerate salt water. Thus the variety of food available to the fauna of the marsh is diminished. More devastating still is the ungluing of the marsh as a result of a decrease in vegetation. Underlying the roots of the living plants is an accumulation of peat—the entangled and matted remains of past vegetation that will have been converted into beds of coal and pockets of oil a million years from now. In some places, Louisiana peat lies twenty feet thick, providing an anchor that helps the marsh withstand the lashings of storms and the pull of currents. But without a protective covering of vegetation, the peat will fast be eaten away.

The destructive process is an unobtrusive one. Surprisingly, the disappearance of eleven thousand acres of marsh each year leaves no gaping hole. Those who live in the marsh see little change from year to year. Only a comparison of old topographical maps with recent aerial photographs gives the perspective of distance. But that kind of perspective does not exist for those who live at the edge of the grass or on the levee of a bayou. These people are aware only of the next day's possibilities—a trapline full of nutrias or a trotline heavy with catfish.

Three

Lonely Paradise

Marsh dwellers like nothing better than to show off their bayous, creveys, and vistas of waving grass. Clifford Stelly did so with an affectionate gruffness and familiarity one morning when I was running traps with him along a trainasse. We came to a section of marsh that looked stricken. The usual thick stands of lovely, golden-hued grass were reduced to a shriveled stubble. Mud flats reflected the morning light with an unhealthy sheen. Rivulets of murky water carved miniature canyons across them. Nutrias had worn highways through this wasteland with their comings and goings, each route marked by myriad pawprints and grooved by draggled tails.

Clifford had warned beforehand. "We gonna see somethin' bad this mornin'," he said in a tone suggesting that both he and the marsh had suffered an insult. "Something happenin' to the marsh that tears it apart."

As he stopped the boat, he spoke accusingly. "See what they done? That's them nutr'a. They done that. There's jus' too many of 'em." He poled the boat's prow into the mud and got out. The mud came to the knees of his hip boots. "Las' year, this was all thick grass here. Thick, thick. An' now, now it all ruined. If we don' trap a lot of them nutr'a outta here, this place gonna be ruined forever. You know what gonna happen if a storm come in here an' the marsh like that? It gonna wipe the mud outta here and make open water, that's what. An' then it will always be open water."

Nutrias and muskrats are both prolific species that breed throughout the year. A muskrat may produce twenty young each year, a nutria around fifteen. Their populations sometimes shoot up to levels that put an unbearable strain on the vegetation, chewing it down to its foundations in the mud. Trappers call such a destructive orgy an "eat-out." Hunger follows, and then disease, and finally a slow, lingering death for thousands of animals. Parts of the marsh where this has happened have been known to stink with decaying bodies. The danger of such grand-scale death is more ammunition that the Louisiana Wildlife and Fisheries Commission uses against animal protection groups. The question is: Isn't a relatively swift death in a trap preferable to an agonizing death by starvation, a certainty, given the fecundity of muskrats and nutrias, if leg-hold traps are ever banned?

In a denuded marsh, the remaining roots will eventually begin sending up shoots. Licking their sores, the remnants of the animal population recover their strength by eating the new grass, reproducing until they become so numerous that another eat-out occurs and the cycle is repeated. Among muskrats, the cycle is known to occur just about every ten years. Nutrias may also be subject to a cycle, but they are so new to the state that no long-term predictions are possible. A local tradition has it that these dull-witted animals were first introduced not far from the Stellys' cabin as part of an extraordinary faunal and floral collection.

To the northeast of the cabin, the marsh is a sea of waving grass, but with one interruption. A forested hillock rises out of the waves, so green and leafy and magically airy, it might be a mirage. Through the feathery tops of the trees on its summit, the chimneyed roof of a mansion is just visible. Below it, fields are spread along the slope in a kind of feudal splendor.

Clifford looks in that direction with awe in his expression. "That's a differen' world over there," he says shyly. "It's like no place else aroun' here. They got trees there, high, high, an' flowers all over. Lord, the egrets that come there are somethin'. They got birds all over an' nutr'a that'll walk right up to you. Talk about money, why ah jus' don' know." His voice trailing off, he shrugs away the image as though the little fiefdom across the marsh was a thing too foreign to understand.

This jewel in the midst of a marsh setting is Avery Island. Not, strictly speaking, an island at all, it does suggest one because of the waves of grass that surround it. A single road links it to the mainland, and a little wooden tollhouse guards access to its abrupt height. The road winds lazily upward through groves of live oaks laden with pendulous epiphytes whose moist shade invites one to linger. Glimpsed between the massive trunks are little houses, each with a front porch. Near the summit the trees give way to a clearing where an ivy-hung old factory building rises from a green lawn. Workers can be seen moving back and forth or resting in the shade, where a thigh-slapping mirth prevails.

Beyond the factory, a lush world of camellias and azaleas unfolds, winding around the hill under the brow of the mansion. Stone laid paths lead downward from sun-dappled lawns to sunken gardens filled with the moist, sensual music of fountains bubbling among moss-covered rocks. One can almost see the naiads emerging from behind screens of shining leaves. Shaded tunnels of wisteria lead to thick groves of feathery bamboo that give way to beds of chrysanthemums. Stone bridges arch lagoons reflecting the oaks and sculptured figures beside them. Egrets strut and ducks paddle in the water, occasionally falling prey to alligators that skulk under the luxuriantly spreading branches.

All this richness sits atop an underground mountain of pure salt. And no ordinary mountain: If it were exposed all the way to its base, it would overtop Mount Everest. South Louisiana is underlain by many such mountains, known locally as "salt domes." Most of them are completely submerged. A few, like Avery Island, poke their heads just above the marsh, providing a base for thick vegetation. The quantity of salt that lies under the gardens on Avery Island could keep the world supplied for centuries to come. Though the island's salt has been mined to a depth of over a thousand feet, that depth hardly more than scratches the surface. Sealed in darkness at the heart of a white world are huge, high-ceilinged rooms carved out around rough supporting pillars, each the size of a city block. The arched portals connecting the galleries are fit for a race of subterranean giants. The floors are as smooth as a ballroom's and the sparkling walls are decorated with multicolored whorls and swirls of salt millions of years old.

A single family descended from John Craig Marsh owns all of this island—the underground world, the gardens, the factory, the workers' houses, and everything else. Locally, its members are known simply as "the family." Marsh was one of several venturesome Yankees who drifted down from the north to explore and exploit the territory acquired in the Louisiana Purchase in 1803. Arriving from Rahway, New Jersey, he bought up part of what was then called *Petite Anse,* French for "Little Cove." How he found the island, or even why he came south, is not known. It is known, however, that some years earlier a deer hunter in the region had discovered salt bubbling to the surface in a spring. Digging down, no matter how deep he went, he found nothing but salt. It is possible that word of this phenomenon had traveled all the way to Rahway and caused young Marsh to prick up his ears and pack his bags.

He apparently didn't mine the salt, but he did clear out a space for himself among the trees, where he built a little house, married, and raised a family. Then another Yankee, Daniel Dudley Avery, got interested in the island. South Louisiana being so flat, it is conceivable that anyone from the north would gravitate toward the nearest hill. Avery arrived via Baton Rouge, where he had served as a circuit judge. After he had bought up the whole island and married Marsh's daughter, people in the vicinity began calling the place Avery's Island instead of Petite Anse.

Once Avery had established himself on the island, the building of the family's compact little empire began. Confederate troops during the Civil War badly needed salt, and the property was sitting on a mountain of it. The judge's son, John Marsh Avery, set out to rediscover the salt spring the deer hunter had found. Within months the family was supplying the entire Confederate Army with salt; in fact, Avery Island was the army's sole source of supply. In those days salt was a far rarer commodity than it is today, and troops on both sides guarded their caches with soldiers and cannons. On Avery Island the salt was dug out of great open pits with pick and shovel and hauled to the mainland by horse and wagon over a log road that half floated on the surface of the marsh.

Before the war began, the family's growing numbers had received a notable addition. Daughters of the island have often married men who chose to settle there rather than whisk their brides away. One such son-in-law was Edmund McIlhenny, a banker from New Orleans. A man with rosy cheeks, an impish mouth, and a long beard that hid his short neck, McIlhenny was a gardener, a gourmand, and a cook who enjoyed experimenting with recipes and spices. A friend who had fought in the Mexican War had brought back for McIlhenny some seeds of the capsicum pepper, which the Indians had long ago domesticated and used as a hot seasoning. McIlhenny welcomed the seeds and planted them in the family vegetable garden.

In 1863, with the South faring badly in the war—New Orleans had fallen, and Union ships controlled the mouth of the Mississippi—Union troops stormed Avery Island and took over the saltworks. The family managed to escape through the marsh and from there made their way to Texas. But on the island the saltworks were destroyed, the buildings burned, and garden left in shambles.

Returning after the war, the family found little growing except a few pepper plants. McIlhenny, who had lost none of his enthusiasm for food, was delighted they had survived. Times were hard; the entire enclave would have to be rebuilt; the saltworks no longer provided any income; and food was scarce. About the only crop that would grow fast was beans. Compared with the prewar luxury of the family table, a diet of beans was hardly inspiring.

McIlhenny thought he could liven it up and began experimenting with his peppers. Using as his laboratory a room in the tower of one of the first reconstructed buildings, he ground up the peppers, fried them, strained and fermented them, and mixed them with salt and vinegar. Having finally developed a flavor to his liking, he tested it on friends from the mainland. They marveled at the rich flamboyance of McIlhenny's sauce and begged him to keep them supplied. Soon he was selling bottles of it to local merchants. As orders began to come in by the thousands, the whole family joined in the business, and McIlhenny patented his recipe under the more piquant name of Tabasco sauce.

With the family's wealth once more established, members of the younger generation could afford to follow their own interests. Edmund McIlhenny's son Edward became a naturalist. It was as though he wanted to clothe the mountain of salt in all the natural beauty the world had to offer. Out of the thin topsoil that covered it, he created the gardens, importing plants from every corner of the world—papyrus from Egypt, papaya trees from South America, timber canes from China, soap trees from India, and camellias from France.

As a young man, he had seized opportunities with a passion. He dropped out of Lehigh University to join a scientific expedition to the Arctic and wound up teaching Eskimo children how to play football on the tundra. Three years later he was leading his own expedition to Point Barrow, Alaska, to collect birds and mammals. While he was there, accident made its contribution to the variety of his gardens. An early winter had pushed ice floes across the Beaufort Sea and locked a Japanese whaling fleet against the Alaskan shore. McIlhenny and his crew rescued the marooned sailors. By way of reward, the Japanese emperor offered the young man a considerable sum of money. He would have none of it. All he wanted from Japan were some Wasi orange trees for his gardens. The wish was granted.

Even as Edward McIlhenny was making something new of the island with greenery from exotic places, he never lost interest in the marsh surrounding it. He spent days wandering by himself with gun in hand and an eye out for ducks and geese. He haunted the levees and had a wave and an ebullient smile for each family of trappers whose shack he passed. They called him Mister Ned, and he knew all their names.

His forays into the marsh were never idle—no mere escape from the boredom of wealth. He was observing nature all the time, and he saw how human greed was disrupting it. He recognized the marsh as a major wintering ground for waterfowl and a nesting area for many other species, among them the snowy egret. Plume hunters were killing off these showy birds with the same blind unconcern as in the Florida Everglades. In Louisiana the egrets were close to extinction. Mister Ned became their rescuer and guardian. Over a section of one of his garden ponds he built a great wire cage where he sequestered seven young snowy egrets. They grew and flourished and at the end of the summer when they had matured, he tore the cage down. The birds flew off to the south for the winter. However pleasant, the experiment had barely put a dent in the slaughter by plume hunters. But the next spring, to the astonishment of all, the egrets returned to the pond and brought mates with them. The descendants of these egrets still return to the island every spring and nest in the same pond. They now number in the thousands.

Between expeditions into the marsh and plantings in the gardens, Edward McIlhenny oversaw the Tabasco business, but at a distance. Sequestered in the family mansion, he wrote detailed scientific articles on such esoteric subjects as eye color in boat-tailed grackles, the predatory inclinations of purple gallinules, and albinism in mockingbirds. He also wrote about skinks and garfish, and in 1935 he published a book on alligators. He kept three alligators as pets. The

slender volume is now recognized by zoologists as a masterpiece of observation.

Given McIlhenny's interest in the natural world beyond his island paradise, it was perhaps inevitable that he should turn to the possibilities of raising nutrias, knowing as he did that the Louisiana climate and the wet environment of the marsh were quite similar to the marshes of Argentina, the nutrias' last stronghold. The animals had been eradicated from other South American countries and from the Caribbean islands that were their ancestral home. The trapping of nutrias had long flourished in Argentina, but from there the skins were sent to Germany for processing, since it was in Berlin that age-old secrets of tanning and cutting had been passed from father to son. Efforts to close the gap between marsh and furrier had been made time and again. In 1882 an ambitious Frenchman began a nutria ranch on the banks of the Loire; later, others built pens in the marshes of central France. Many of the animals escaped, to thrive for a time in the wild.

The first nutria ranch in this country was begun in Elizabeth City, California, in 1889. Why there, so distant from Berlin, is not known. Something went wrong with the operation and the pens fell into disarray. The creeks and swampy areas nearby proliferated with descendants of the escapees until, in the 1940s, farmers exterminated them because they ate crops. By 1932 the Depression had produced a spate of backyard nutria farms through the Midwest and along the eastern seaboard, none of them really more than a sideline, though promoters guaranteed one could make a fortune. Hundreds of nutrias also came into Louisiana as a result of such schemes, to be added to household menageries along with chickens, pigs, goats, and a few cows. No fortunes were made, and many of the nutrias ended up in the marsh.

In 1938 McIlhenny put in an order for some nutrias from a New Orleans fur dealer, one A. Bernstein, who advertised himself as a "direct receiver of fine French settlement minks, raccoons, and muskrats." Evidently Bernstein also did a considerable business in live nutrias, and McIlhenny had to wait his turn before his order could be filled. The twenty animals he finally received had been shipped from a nutria farm in New Jersey. They were accompanied by Bernstein's own inimitable instructions:

> Start making you [sic] fence on the lot you showed me next to the canal and have plenty fresh water from swimming pool. Feed them with sweet potatoes, cabbage and carrots. Don't feed potatoes unless they are sound. No rottens. Stale bread can be used, only stale bread is good for them. I had a hard time trading with the two partners. I had other parties interested in buying them, but I promised you last year, so I worked the deal through to get them for you. The lot you showed me have some muskrats on. I want to see if there is any chance to crossbread [sic] the muskrats with the nutrias. That would be the greatest experiment yet, but you must have them inclosed, otherwise you will not get results.

Nutrias began appearing in the marsh around Avery Island shortly after some of them escaped from McIlhenny's pen. It was assumed that these were his former charges. Whether they were or not will never be known.

About this time, the reputation of nutrias as voracious eaters of vegetation spread over the state. Exploiting the trait, promoters advertised the animals as nature's own cure for the plague of water hyacinths that was beginning to clog the waterways of the South. The hyacinths themselves had been unintentionally introduced by Japanese businessmen who gave away specimens of these prolific and graceful flowering plants during the 1884 Cotton States Exposition at New Orleans. As it turned out, nutrias would eat the hyacinth plants only if nothing better was at hand. One result of the latest nutria-selling gimmick was that many of the animals were loosed in bayous and canals throughout the state.

They were not popular in Louisiana during those early years. Sugarcane growers suffered huge losses as a result of the damage inflicted by those shocking orange teeth. Rice farmers made the angry discovery that nutrias were draining their fields as they burrowed through levees that held in the water. Automobile drivers complained that the carcasses of nutrias littering the roads constituted a safety hazard.

Trappers had still another complaint. They said the nutrias they found in their traps were giving them a rash; they called it nutria itch. Health officials passed off the complaint as no more than a gripe against intruders whose skins were at first considered worthless. Laboratory tests showed, however, that many of the nutrias carried the blood fluke, *Schistosoma mansoni,* a parasite that can cause a minor form of schistosomiasis, known as swimmer's itch.

A second complaint lodged by trappers was more serious: Nutrias were cutting down the populations of muskrats, the established fur animal of the marsh. There could be no doubt that this was true. If Wildlife and Fisheries Commission officials now hesitate to accuse the nutria, that may be a reflection of the animal's revenue-accumulating powers. Clifford Stelly is one of many trappers who express bitter sentiments against nutrias. "Used to be ah could bring in three hundred 'rats a day," he once told me, "but them nutr'as done run 'em outta here. Ah'm lucky if ah get thirty a week."

The trappers' protests against nutrias were largely ignored, but those of the farmers were listened to. Sugarcane was now becoming big business and Louisiana rice growers were organizing into cooperatives—unlike the trappers, who merely roamed the marsh, solitary anachronisms. The result was that in 1958 the nutria, an animal that had never come to Louisiana on its own four feet, was placed by legislative vote on the "outlawed quadruped" list and joined the ranks of coyotes, foxes, and rats as vermin. The sentence was death, any-where, any time, and in unlimited numbers. Thousands fell victim to poison, farmers' pitchforks, and wandering boys with .22-caliber rifles.

It was economics that saved the species. In 1945, when a good nu-tria pelt brought only fifty cents, trappers did not even bother to skin most of the nutrias that came their way. They just hit the animal over the head and left it to die. But fur dealers eventually recognized the value Europeans placed on nutrias, and as encouragement, the price they paid to trappers went up. Trappers responded with so many nutria skins that the price dropped again. It finally bottomed out at one dollar per skin. A decade later, European pelt handlers and furriers began to realize that the nutria was an established species in Louisiana. Prices began to rise, and the nutria, now legally sanctified, could be killed only during the winter trapping season.

In the 1961–62 season, for the first time, the nutria outdid the muskrat in the greater number of pelts taken. Since then it has not once relinquished its lead and probably never will. During the 1976–77 season, trappers sold almost 1,300,000 nutria skins, com-pared with just over 965,000 muskrat pelts. Nutria pelts made up well over one-third of all the skins harvested in the state. The other animals, besides muskrats, included raccoons, otters, skunks, foxes, bobcats, opossums, minks, and coyotes.

The proliferation of nutrias is largely responsible for making Loui-siana this country's leading fur-producing state, far surpassing those northern states whose snow-blanketed pine forests and icy streams have traditionally been associated with furs. Since 1964, the marsh and the bayous of Louisiana have accounted for an average of about 40 percent of the total fur harvest. In some years, they have produced as much as 65 percent of the total.

This contribution to statistics has not improved the animal's repu-tation in the eyes of trappers, notwithstanding the high price paid for its skin. In 1977–78 a prime nutria pelt brought in $8.00, whereas buyers paid around $4.50 for a prime muskrat pelt. However, in the time a trapper is able to skin, scrap, dry, and stretch one nutria pelt, he can complete the same process with three muskrat skins. The trapper thus loses $5.50 on every nutria he catches—providing, that is, he is able to trap the extra muskrat. But this he is not always able to do, so indiscriminate have the territorial acquisitions of the nutria become. The two species can and do live side by side, but not frequently and not over a long period. Compared with muskrats, the dainty homebodies of the marsh, nutrias are swaggering ruffians that trample over everyone's front lawns. In the face of this abuse, muskrats sometimes opt for moving to better neighborhoods; more frequently, though, they remain in the old neighborhood and either give in to the disturbance outside their lodges or starve to death.

Four

At the Gulf's Edge

Seventy-five miles east and south of the Stellys' cabin, the marsh begins to slip into the Gulf of Mexico, appearing to consist of bits and pieces, an islet here and there in a widening expanse of water. The bayous are wider and more meandering, the lakes bigger, and the winter winds fiercer—screaming across the marsh with a cold unconcern, flattening the grass, churning the shallow water into angry breakers, and keeping trappers in their cabins for days at a time.

When Jim Daisy is shut up inside his cabin on Buckskin Bayou, his fingers begin drumming wherever they come to rest, their steady rhythm mocking the gusts that wrench at the cabin. When I saw Jim toward the end of one trapping season, he had not been able to run his traps for two days. His usually vibrant eyes had gone dead. The skin around his jaws was slack. He kept putting on and then taking off his red baseball cap, laying it on the table beside him and then putting it back on again.

"Doggone it, I'm just goin' to have to start cooking. That's what I'm gonna do. I cain't run my traps in this weather. I gotta do something." His eyes widened and he spread his hands, palms up, as if to say that all alternatives had been exhausted.

"Willie, go out an' get me some oysters, will ya. That' what I'm going to do, fry us up a bunch of oysters. An' if it's still blowin' like this tomorrow, I'll do us some catfish in sauce piquante, like those Cajuns do it. I like to cook, but, you know, I jus' don' have the time for it. I do it more now since the wife passed away, but I jus' don' have the time when I'm runnin' my traps. But with this weather, I jus' gotta do somethin'. I get restless, you know what I mean?"

Jim and his two sons, Willie and Dwight, are muskrat trappers not by choice, but rather because muskrats—along with some raccoons—frequent the marsh where they set their traplines. Muskrats can tolerate saline water, whereas nutrias shy away from it. The marsh on the edge of the Gulf is thus one of the last strongholds in Louisiana for muskrats.

Jim doesn't really like trapping. He does it mostly because he wants to be in the marsh and the three-month-long season gives him a break from oystering, the occupation for which he has a real affection. Certainly there is little economic reason for him to continue trapping. A good season will bring him $12,000 worth of muskrat skins, compared with the $60,000 he usually makes from oystering— enough so he can buy a new car and truck most years, keep his three worn oysters luggers in repair, maintain his little house in the community of Bayou du Large, and support three of his four children plus a number of other relatives.

"I jus' traps fer the fun of it," he told me, "an' to give my oysters a rest. But you know, if I couldn't come out here, I think I'd go plumb crazy."

Jim, as much as Clifford Stelly, sees the marsh as the center of his world. A few years ago he was fortunate enough to take an all-expense-paid two-week trip to Germany with the man who buys his furs. Some German fur processors were courting the buyer and suggested that he bring a few trappers with him. Jim's memories of the trip focus on cars and food to such an extent that it's difficult to know what he thought of Germany other than through these two criteria. "You know, I never drove so fast in my whole life and I never ate so much steak before. They don' go slower'n a hundred miles an hour on those highways, even in traffic. No sir, I never seen nothing like it. An' that steak was out of this world."

We went outside, feeling the marsh wind sting our faces, to watch Willie, a sinewy twenty-five-year-old with dazzlingly blue eyes and a blond beard that never seems to grow beyond a scraggly mat. He was kneeling over the bayou on a boardwalk that led to a wharf, reaching down into the frigid water to pluck oysters from the bottom, where Jim had seeded a colony a couple of years earlier. Now, when anybody in the family wants oysters, they are there to be scooped up.

Next to Willie, a partially filled bucket contained three dozen of them.

"Com'on, Willie. We're gettin' hungry," his father said, with the singsong intonation he always uses when he is feeling edgy and trying to conceal the fact.

Willie's only response was a casual turn of his head toward the east, where storm clouds barricaded the horizon. He stared at them intently for a few moments, his big eyes wide and rimmed with an irritation of his own. "I buhlieve if this keeps up, we're gonna have to run those traps anyway," he said in a high-pitched voice whose incredulous tone was meant to counteract his father. "I bet I got a lot of 'rats out there. I haven't runned my traps fer three days now."

Dwight, a teenager still swaddled in a roll of puppy fat, beamed with calculated innocence as he said, "I'm not goin' out there tomorrow. I'm gonna set myself inside next to the heater, fill 'er up with wood, an' jus' watch the TV all day."

Jim turned on Dwight, his tone jocular but brimming with impatience. "You better git out there tomorrow. You jus' got yourself a new car an' got a note to pay off now, boy. No one's gonna pay it for you."

Dwight shrugged, his innocence crumpling to a hurt smile. The tension died as Willie stood up. The bucket was full. Jim pulled an oyster knife out of his pocket and began shucking, seemingly with no more than the amount of effort one might expend in shelling peas. Big, fat globs of oyster meat fell into a bowl. "Now these here oysters are sassy," Jim gloated. "Lookit this, Willie. See how fat this one is? Yessir, if they got any salt in 'em, we'll be doin' all right." The shucking and the sight of the rich meat was therapeutic for Jim. His tight shoulders relaxed, and the rigidly held lines on his face softened.

A smile played across Willie's lips. "I buhlieve you were an oyster 'fore you was borned. I never seen anyone talk 'bout oysters like you. You're worse'n Willie Junior. That boy's gonna turn into an oyster. You give him an oyster reef an' he's never gonna stop eatin' 'em."

In the cabin, Jim prepared to fry the oysters with a diligence that the mood of a few moments ago would not have permitted. With quick, sure movements he opened cabinet doors and emptied the contents of the shelves onto the counter near the stove. Then he lined them all up in order and stood back for a moment surveying cans and boxes, hands on his hips, the baseball cap askew.

As he rolled each oyster in corn flour before laying it delicately on a plate, he began talking about his wife. Perhaps the role he was assuming, one that had been hers exclusively, brought back a pang of memory only talk could relieve.

"The wife taught me how to do oysters. Ya know, a lot of people don' know how to fry oysters. They come out greasy an' heavy-like. But if you got yer grease hot, why, they're as light an' crisp as anything.

"She used to do all the cookin'. Now, I gotta do it. The boys, they don' like to cook. When Rachel comes out here—she's my daughter, the older one—she does the cookin', but she don' like it out here too good. It's too quiet out here for her. Me. I like that. But the trouble is they don't got a telephone out here, you know what I mean, an' boy, she cain't keep off that phone."

"Hey," piped Willie, from the picnic table in the middle of the room where he had been worrying a splinter in his hand, "ya know what Rachel tol' me she was gonna do? She's gonna go on a seafood diet; she's gonna eat all the food she can see."

Without a pause, he hunched over his hand again. Jim laughed softly, as if he thought the remark funny, but also, by implication, embarrassing. Dwight smiled. He sat on a broken-down and squashed couch near one corner of the room, hands behind his head, a dreamy expression in his eyes, legs sprawled out so that his feet nearly touched the wood stove where logs were spluttering. Behind him, four double beds with sagging mattresses were partitioned off from the rest of the cabin by blankets hanging on a rope. Every few minutes the cabin trembled as the wind gave it a broadside gust.

Pages from magazines showing European landscapes and New England foliage decorated the walls. "See that pi'ture?" Jim asked, pointing to one of an Alpine village. His eyes lit up. "The wife put that there. She liked mountains. An' see these cabinets here? She spent two days puttin' paper on 'em. I sat right here watchin' her standin' up there for hours at a time to do it good. The next day, she was gone. It seems jus' like yestid'y, like she oughta come back and take up right where she stopped."

Silence filled the room. Willie and Dwight looked at their father with tolerant understanding, but as if they already were too familiar with such reminiscences. Jim looked down at the floor and pulled his baseball cap further onto his head, as though to keep the past from spilling out over the present.

*   *   *

Out in the marsh the next day, with the wind sweeping down upon us, Jim tugged at the red hat in relentless defiance of the gusts. The marsh grass bent almost horizontal and shimmered in the cold morning light. The dampness coursed over my body, layered though it was in sweaters and protected by a slicker. My legs were the coldest; clammy rubber hip boots trapped the moisture in the air along with my own sweat. Hip boots are essential in the marsh, especially for a muskrat trapper.

We were in Jim's mudboat, an eighteen-foot skiff with an ancient sixteen-horsepower engine planted amidships and a propeller fastened close against the bottom. Most trappers use such boats, practically all of them homemade. Their engines have been hoisted out of abandoned cars or trucks or, as in this instance, a lawn mower. The beauty of such craft is that their inboard motors and propeller arrangement allow them to churn through bayous and channels that are half mud and half water. Jim stood just forward of the roaring engine, the steering stick grasped in one hand and the choke lever in the other. A cigarette dangled from his mouth, one of an unending series that adds up to three packs a day.

Muskrat trapping is an arduous business, probably imposing more physical strain than any other marsh occupation. Unlike nutrias, raccoons, otters, or minks, muskrats frequent a section of marsh away from the waterways. A trapper must trudge into the heart of the marsh when he tracks down this small and delicate animal.

It is difficult to walk in the marsh under any conditions, but particularly so in areas where muskrats live. Their tunnels zigzag everywhere under the grass and mud, and the roofs are fragile—a few inches of peat and roots that do not support much weight. A trapper can hardly escape breaking into a tunnel no matter how careful he is in jumping from one grass clump to another. Such a misstep plunges him abruptly into a nightmarish ooze that slithers about his thighs.

A trapper like Jim has learned to walk over such terrain. He does so with loose knees. When he feels himself falling, his bent knees slump to the mud, breaking the downward passage by the added resistance. Even this expertise does not make the work much less exhausting. It was surprising to me that a man like Jim, long past his prime and with lungs laboring under the effects of too much tobacco, could spend hours in this lonely and treacherous landscape.

Tunneling occupies most of a muskrat's nocturnal hours. Daytime is for sleeping in a warm grass lodge, but the night is for work. The tunnels serve two purposes: to free the tender animals from the predations of raccoons, foxes, hawks, and owls, and to provide access to the succulent roots that are the mainstay of their diet. Burrowing here and there as they feed, muskrats open up a complex network of interconnecting tunnels whose windings only they can follow. Most of the tunnels quickly fill with water, and muskrats must frequently stop their labors and pop through to the surface for breaths of air. They use these same holes as entrances into the world above the surface and for quick exits from it when they sense danger.

Muskrat trappers usually encircle each colony with a string of traps. At the beginning of the season, the circle is large and loose. But as the months go by it is constricted to form an ever-tightening noose. Jim had set three traplines, each with about a hundred traps. As the season was near its end, the circles were tight, with a diameter of no more than forty yards. To be successful, muskrat traps are set in the most frequently used tunnels and holes. Very often it is not at all obvious which these are, for signs of muskrats—pawprints, remains of gnawed roots, and droppings—surround nearly every hole. A trapper's ability to select the right ones out of the chaos in front of him amounts to a sixth sense concerning the ways of muskrats.

"You jus' feels where they're gonna be," Jim says. "I don' know how I do it. Mebbe it's 'cause I been doin' it all my life. Sometimes

I'm wrong, but when they're here, I usually knows where they're at."

Jim talked constantly as he moved across the marsh toward the first trapline, poking his killing stick ahead of him to test the firmness of the ground. Occasionally his body twisted awkwardly as one of his feet broke through a tunnel roof. "It takes a while to learn to walk in this marsh. You take little Willie Junior, there. Now, he's twelve years old an' he can walk real good now, but last year, I thought he would about drowned when I took him trappin'. He was stumblin' all over the place.

"That was right in back of the cabin, there. Willie set up a trapline for him an' he went out near every day runnin' it. He did good too. He made near two hundred dollars. That's the way everybody learns to trap. Now, you take Dwight there, he didn't trap till about three years ago when he dropped outta school an' started runnin' traps. He still ain't too good at it, but he's learnin'."

We were approaching the first trapline. The white flags on the stakes up ahead made a rough and desolate circle. At the first trap, I watched Jim reach into the hole and drag out the chain. A slime-covered and stiffly frozen muskrat was in the trap. "I knew I'd get you. I tol' myself when I put that set there, 'Some 'rat gonna be doin' some high steppin' tonight and step right into that trap.' An' look what we got. I knewed I was right."

When his traps are full, Jim's conversation is between himself and his marsh world. "Com'on outta there, Josephine. You knew I'd getcha. You didn't need to go way back there on that hole and try to hide from me."

At another trap, he paused and shifted his red hat. "Now, this here trap's empty, but I know what I'm gonna do. I'm gonna put it over here in this here hole. I smells a 'rat in here an' when the moon is out tonight, that 'rat's gonna come to James, won't ya."

Halfway around one of the traplines, he stopped and stiffened. The muskrat in the trap before him had its soft underbelly gnawed away, the intestines trailing into the marsh. "A coon done that," Jim said, his voice suddenly glum with a hint of nervousness in it. "That's what happens if ya don' come out here every day. Them coons'll help themselves. Ya cain't blame'm, I guess. Mebbe we'll ketch him further on. They get sloppy when they start sniffin' aroun' traps."

The raccoon had attacked the muskrats in the next ten traps, going for the belly of each one. As Jim came up to the remains of each, he muttered something about the loss. Suddenly he shouted,

"Hey, lookit there. There he is." Several traps further ahead, the white flag on a pole jerked frantically and the masked face of a young raccoon bobbed up and down between the clumps of grass. The animal paced back and forth and tugged uselessly at its painful tether.

"One thing about a coon," Jim said excitedly as we plunged toward it, "no matter how young they is, you cain't let 'em out of a trap. Lookit the teeth on that animal. You think nutria got sharp teeth. You oughta see what those can do." The lips curled back and two rows of needle-sharp teeth probed forward in quick jerks. Jim raised his club and brought it down. The blow struck squarely but the raccoon merely jumped away and glared. Jim took a step toward it and struck again, this time splitting the animal's scalp so that blood poured down over its eyes and muzzle. The raccoon ran back and forth as far as the chain would allow it, now in a blind panic. Jim hit it three more times before its legs crumpled, and another three before it died. Sweat ran glistening from his brow by the time he came down with the last blow. He was quiet. All he said was, "Well, at least he paid for all them 'rats he ate up." He picked up the limp and bloody animal and slung it over his shoulder.

He finished running the three traplines by midafternoon. Sixty muskrats lay in the bottom of the boat, their bodies frozen into tortured poses. "I believe those 'rats like me," Jim yelled over the roar of the engine. His eyes sparkled and his mouth opened to release a throaty laugh that sounded like a valve letting go. "Yessir, I do think my reputation out there is spreadin'. I think I got 'em curious and they're comin' over to my traps to see what's goin' on."

Willie and Dwight were washing their muskrats on the wharf, running their hands up and down the stiff bodies in firm but gentle strokes to squeeze the water out of the thick fur. As with the Stellys, the daily reunion initiates a ritual of recounting adventures, observations, successes, and failures out in the marsh. But the conversation drags as the skinning begins. The three figures huddle over their benches, a pile of muskrats beside each, fatigue seeming to eclipse all spontaneity. The only verbal accompaniment to the sounds of cutting and scraping has to do with hunger, the next day's weather, and the need for sleep.

Muskrat trappers work for their pelts; nutria trappers just harvest them. Anyone can trap a nutria. The animal's almost perfect adaptation to the Louisiana marsh has not only altered the economics of trapping, but also changed the occupation from one requiring patience and a feeling for the marsh to a commercial enterprise. In the old days, trappers were constantly challenged by muskrats, minks, and otters, wary animals that skirted the scent of man and honed his power of observation.

The influx of nutrias brought still another change. Trappers now rely on motorboats rather than working the marsh by foot or pirogue, the name first given a dugout canoe used by Indians but now more often applied to a double-ended, narrow-beam dory nailed together out of plywood and cypress. Because nutrias can be trapped from the edge of a marsh's waterways, trappers scarcely need to leave their boats when running traplines. But nutrias are heavy animals, far too heavy for a pirogue to support in any numbers. Most nutria trappers now merely cruise along a bayou or trainasse in their outboards, plucking animals from the traps on the banks as though they were so many pumpkins in a field.

Outboards and nutrias—the two newcomers to the marsh—also deaden a trapper's inclination to spend time there. Many of the state's forty-five hundred licensed trappers now stay year round in their homes at the edge of the marsh and run their traplines as a daily routine, dragging their outboards behind their cars each morning to a public launching site. Commuting like this makes trapping seem more and more to be just another job.

Rare is the trapper today whose life is unshaken by the accessories of the times. The outboard, now viewed by most people as essential to marsh life, is only one of these. The garble of the television and CB radio intrude upon the nighttime calm of cabin life; electricity generators and discarded butane tanks and refrigerators dot the environs of marsh cabins like new species of shrubbery. But exceptions, however anachronistic, do exist.

Wilson and Azalea Verrett are known throughout the marsh, if only to the extent that people have heard about them and have a feeling for them. "Them's the old couple that lives way out by Lake de Cade," you might hear in one town. In another, someone will say with a hint of disbelief, "Now you take Wilson there; he don't use nothing but a pirogue to get himself around the marsh. That's the way they used to do it."

From a distance, the cabin the couple lives in during the trapping season looks so fragile you might think a blow from a flyswatter would knock it over. No more than a speck on the marsh's textured surface, it is coated in black tar paper, has two windows, and clings to the edge of a canal an oil company once dredged and then abandoned. The fragile appearance is deceptive. Wilson crafted the cabin for strength, putting cypress uprights six feet down into the soil of the levee and binding them into a unit with an intricate mesh of beams and planks. The walls are solid cypress, the slightly pitched roof is heavy, and the two doors fit like a book's cover. There is a touch of whimsy in the crooked stovepipe angling from the roof and wearing a conical hat.

Besides an upright rectangle of corrugated tin that serves as the outhouse, there is a fur shed, covered in tar paper like the cabin. I found Wilson and Azalea behind this shed, skinning nutrias and muskrats. Wilson is a tall man with watery eyes, high cheekbones, a creased and sun-bronzed skin. Beside him, Azalea is girlish in looks and manner despite her sixty-odd years; her mouth and eyes constantly crinkle into smiles. Wilson remains formal, as if needing a reason to show animation.

"If I had knowed you was coming," said Azalea in a chirping sing-song that suggested, as did her quick movements, something in common with the red-winged blackbirds that hung around the camp, "I would have done you some biscuits."

Wilson skins his nutrias without any conveniences. That was the first thing I noticed that set him apart from other trappers. Whereas most trappers fasten the hindquarters down, with either chocks or rope, and then pull the skin over the head, Wilson merely steps on the tail and back legs and gives a mighty heave. "When I gotta tie down a daid nutr'a to skin 'im," he says, "then it's time to move outta the marsh."

Day after day, the old couple work side by side. Azalea sets her traps close to the cabin; Wilson's are far out among the meandering channels. They each use a pirogue to get about, propelling the ill-balanced boat with a push-pole—a long pole forked at one end so as to provide some resistance against the mud.

Wilson push-poles his pirogue from ten to fifteen miles every day. It is grueling work. Some days he must fight winds howling in from the Gulf. When the wind shifts to the north, it pushes the water out of the marsh, leaving only three or four inches in the trainasses—a shallow ooze that grabs tenaciously at a boat's underside. He is a pic-

turesque figure during these struggles, or standing in silhouette against the rising sun, starting off in the morning to run his traps, or returning in the sunset of late afternoon. The high grass beside the narrow channels hides his lower body, and he looks like a remnant of the past as he glides through the marsh. He slowly lifts his pole, so that it looks like an extension of his arms, and leans forward stiff-bodied, delicately sinking the fork in the water ahead of him. The casual deliberation of the movements boils over into a downward lunge and a forward push, the muscles of his broad shoulders bulging with the effort as the light boat shoots forward, leaving behind a pool of churned mud.

Wilson has a motorboat, a "motor pirogue" as he calls it, but he rarely uses it, although if he did his work would take only a quarter as long. "Ah was borned usin' a pirogue an' ah'll die usin' one." Tradition is his standard defense, although sometimes he will buttress it a little: "An' besides, ya cain't trust them motors nowadays. I don' know what they make 'em outta, but they fall apart like they was glued together. Now, whadd'ya think would happen to me if I was out in the marsh with a broken motor pirogue an' a storm came up? Why, that would be it, it would. Now, with a push-pole, you can see your storm comin' an' make for shelter real fast."

The unreliability of motors is always a worry in the marsh, but storms do not strike every day, and when they do, they are not always death-dealing. A man in a pirogue with a push-pole could hardly outpace a storm racing across the marsh. Tradition not only supports Wilson against the uncertainties of a changing marsh world, but also lets him spend hours setting his traps. He covers the metal jaws with a thin layer of mud, which he sprinkles with water to wash away any human trace. He still tries to trap otters, the marsh's most elusive animals, and will endlessly probe the levees in search of tracks and slides. Many trappers don't even think about going after otters. Occasionally an otter will stumble into a trap and the owner is thirty or forty dollars richer for it. Wilson has more success; during the 1977–78 trapping season, he took over twenty otters. But for most trappers, all the nutrias in the marsh make it not worth the trouble to skin one otter when they can skin five nutrias in the same length of time.

Azalea's short trapline produces five to ten muskrats most days. She skins these intermittently during the mornings, but the chore is a painful one for her. Arthritis, the bane of marsh life, has partially crippled her fingers and taken the strength out of her arms. After skinning an animal, her hands ache for hours at a time. She rests from the task by attending to what she loves to do—cleaning the cabin, preparing meals, and taking care of her dog Tommy, whom she calls "my baby." He is twelve years old, black and white, half Chihuahua and half some unidentifiable breed, and he now sleeps almost twenty-four hours a day. A few years ago he suffered a stroke that left him partially paralyzed. When he moves, he hobbles about, wavering feebly, and at the sight of this Azalea will gather him into her arms and cover his head with kisses.

She sweeps out the little cabin three or four times a day. But as she does so, she keeps a wary eye out for Tommy in his box and for Wilson in the marsh. I think of her in a typical pose—standing against the door jamb, broom in hand, a floppy bonnet on her head, gazing out over the marsh with a singsong "Where's that Weelson gone to now? I saw him push-polin' over there awhile back an' now I don' see him nowheres. I wonder where he's at." Her voice has an edge of worry. The wrinkles in her face seem to deepen momentarily, and her eyes look tired as she goes back to her sweeping.

The cabin has three rooms—a combined living room and kitchen plus two bedrooms. The walls separating the rooms are of quarter-inch plywood painted a hospital green. A flowered linoleum in light green and red, which Azalea proudly refers to as her "rug," covers the floor. The furniture is spartan—three or four wood-slat armchairs and a table, all painted dark green, the table covered with a green-and-white-checked cloth, a kerosene lamp in the middle. A kerosene stove, gleaming white with delicately curved legs, stands in one corner, framed by pots and pans that hang from the wall behind it. There are not enough of them for Azalea, and she often prods Wilson to buy her more. "Weelson, he don' like to buy nothin', him. He could live with one plate an' that's all," she chirps, tilting her head with a flirtatious glance at Wilson, who sits in his rocking chair, his legs crossed daintily, knee over knee, a teasing look about his mouth.

"Ah'll tell you one thing," his retort begins, "you spend money on a set of pots these days, an' you'll be too poor to put anything in 'em." Anything slightly foreign to Wilson's narrow world must be regarded suspiciously, sniffed out, and closely watched. "We don' need nothin' more out here. We got everything. We eats good food an' we got a roof over our haids an' we got plenty of friends. If a man don' have friends, he's got himself some trouble. Ah'll tell you what. One time I was out runnin' ma traps, an' the sheriff comes up with his shotgun. He was huntin' ducks. I ses to him, 'This here is ma lan' an' you got no right on it an' you can jus' take yerself off it.' He wouldn't move an' so I popped him one right smack in the face. He wen' over like a cut tree, he did. They come an' take me to court, but I got some friends who knowed the judge, an' he let me off I never seen that sheriff 'roun' here agin, no sir."

Wilson warms to his stories, his bravado expanding the longer he talks. The rhythmic movement of his rocking chair seems to help, also, to keep the stories coming. At night when the glow of the kerosene lantern just reveals the fatigue in his eyes, he rocks back and forth, a Lucky Strike in one hand and a demitasse in the other. Each story pits Wilson against the world either of people or of animals. It is as though in the isolation of the marsh he had evolved into a different species.

"Ah'll tell you one thing, you cain't trust none of them sports 'roun' here," is the introduction to one set of stories. "It's all the dope floatin' aroun'. It's gittin' to their haids. People don' care about nothin' anymore 'cept themselves. Jes' las' week, I had an otter in a trap right 'crost the other side of the canal. Ah seed him thrashin' aroun' an' was gonna go an' git him when three sports come up in a motorboat an' start circlin' aroun' like they was gonna take 'im. Well, ah'll tell you what I done. Ah took ma shotgun, a sixteen-gauge it was, an' I runned out onto the wharf an' I started yellin' at 'em. I said, 'Com'on, ah dare you to tech that animal, in fact, ah'll double dare you, 'cause if ya do, I gonna blow yer haids off.' Well, you shoulda seen them tear outta there." Wilson rocks back, his bony face broken by a grin. His courage, with age staring him in the face, is touching.

An evening conversation invariably turns to alligator hunting, memories of which make Wilson glow. Most trappers speak of it in the same way, their voices rising as though to do justice to the gnashing jaws and lashing tail of that foe. Toward the end of the last century, when the price of alligator skins began to increase, hunters went into the marsh by the hundreds. They cruised the bayous and channels by night with ready rifles and lard lanterns. The eyes of alligators gleamed from the tops of the levees, where the beasts lay in wait for prey and made easy targets.

As more and more alligator skins went into bags, belts, and shoes, hunters probed deeper into the marsh, often blundering onto a reptile's territory. An adult alligator makes its den in the bank of a channel or in a water-filled hollow it carves underneath the floor of the marsh. A den may consist of a soggy and winding tunnel as much as forty feet long and down as much as fifteen feet below the marsh. Whatever alligators remained isolated in the middle of the marsh now hid in their underwater chambers at the slightest disturbance. Although many hunters probably gave up seeking their quarry when the levees at night no longer glowed with eyes, the more determined ones took to snatching alligators right out of their homes with long poles. Wilson was one of these.

Alligator poling was an arduous and patience-straining task. It made some proud reputations; it destroyed others—some quite literally. The hunter would spend days in the marsh, jumping from hummock to hummock, until he stumbled upon a muddy trail of clawed prints, littered with the remains of fish and waterfowl. Sometimes the musky odor of a bull alligator hung over the trail leading to a 'gator hole or the mouth of a den. The hunter carried a shovel and an ax, or a rifle, but his most important equipment was two poles, each about twenty feet long and one tipped with an iron hook for probing through the den's roof to feel out the alligator. After striking an animal's back, the hunter would shovel away the marsh muck until he broke through the roof. With the brown water still hiding the alligator, more intimate probing would begin—this time with the hooked pole, which gradually moved toward the animal's head until its manipulator judged it to be under the jaw. A mighty jerk would secure the alligator, but would often send it into a rage, depending upon weather conditions—during cold days the alligator's lowered body temperature would make it lethargic, but during hot weather the reptile's tail would whip through the muddy water and into the air, crumbling the walls of its den and caving in the remaining roof. The hunter would look down into a miniature amphitheater where mud, water, and air swirled in horrible fury until a bullet or ax blade between the eyes subdued the victim.

Wilson enjoys recounting stories of the tense moments just after hooking an alligator. "Ah'll tell you what," is the refrain he begins with, in a studied rocking back and forth, the light flickering off his chiseled face. "Ah was huntin' one time with another fella and we hooked a 'gator an' began to pull. He wouldn't budge. The other fella said it was a log, but I knowed it was a big 'gator. We pulled an'

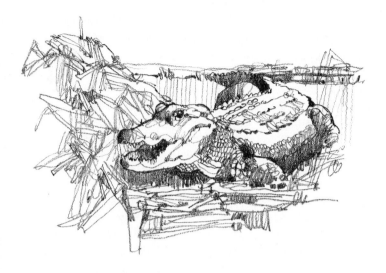

pulled an' he wouldn't budge. I tol' him to go get us some help, an'
another person came, but that 'gator wouldn't move. Then I got ma
shotgun an' loaded her with buckshot shell. I knowed he was too
deep under the mud for the buckshot to git at him, but ah thought
the noises would shake him. Ah was right. Ah held the end of the
barrel a couple of inches from the mud an' let 'er go. That 'gator
came outta there like a waterspout, mud flyin' all over the place. Ah
didn't have my rifle with me. I always killed ma 'gators with a knife.
After he slowed down a bit, I jumped right into that hole up toward
the head. Ah knowed that tail woulda broke me in half. Well, as
soon as I could, I stuck him in the spot right back of the haid. That
was it. He was daid."

Such stories usually end with Wilson rocking toward the kerosene
lamp, his face suddenly visible as though to give substance to his
tales. The words dwindle off into the stillness of the night, with a
reprise or two: "No sir, ah never shot an alligator in ma whole life.
But ah killed thousands of 'em with ma pocketknife."

The days of poling formally ended in 1967, when the federal government classified the alligator as an endangered species. That
brought all hunting for it to an end, although in recent years Louisiana has permitted very limited hunting on an experimental basis. But
for all practical purposes poling ended years before the federal classi-
fication, so scarce had alligators become. Ironically, the hunting had
given marsh ecology a sharp twist that wrung a new industry out of

the grass and mud. The height of the season was early fall, when the marsh grass was still heavy and tall. During the last years of poling, hunters took to burning the grass in dry periods to facilitate their more difficult search for alligator holes and dens. In the late fall and winter many of these same hunters trapped minks, otters, raccoons, and foxes, as they had always done. Within the space of a few seasons, a new animal began to appear in their traps. It was small, had a ratlike tail and gray and brown fur that was soft and thick. Some trappers didn't know what it was; they had never seen one before. Others recognized it as a muskrat.

Biologists had long known that muskrats lived in isolated pockets in Louisiana, but were mystified by the increase. Some speculated that something was happening in the lakes and rivers to the north—some environmental change that had driven the animals south. But the muskrats in Louisiana were small, weighing no more than two pounds. In the north, the average animal weighed over three pounds. It didn't make sense that a species would or even could become so much smaller just by moving south. Also, the skeletal structure of the head varied between the northern and the Louisiana muskrats. Such differences forced scientists to acknowledge that the muskrats in the Louisiana marsh were a distinct variety of the species that inhabits most of North America (with the exception of Newfoundland, where a separate species lives) and warranted a distinct scientific name. The Louisiana muskrat was labeled *Ondatra zibethicus rivalicus,* as distinguished from its more common and widespread northern cousin, *Ondatra zibethicus zibethicus.* The name *rivalicus* was based on a footnote to Louisiana's history: An eighteenth-century French explorer had noticed the animals swimming in the bayous and had facetiously written that one day settlers would have to compete with muskrats for space there.

Why the increase in their numbers? The natural assumption was that the once numerous alligators had kept a tight rein on any substantial proliferation of muskrats. But something else had been happening. Whereas for years the alligator population had been dwindling, that of the muskrat had shot up all of a sudden. Someone examined the muskrats' diet and discovered that their favorite food was three-cornered grass, a common marsh species named for the triangular shape of its blades, that grows in a great waving blanket of green. Horny little seedpods cling to the tips of the blades and jostle up and down. It had been this blanket of grass that the alligator hunters burned away. In a matter of weeks, tender new shoots would spring from the charred remains, and muskrats would abandon their typical diet of roots to go on an eating spree that produced glossy coats, regular breeding cycles, and lodges full of furry kits.

It is thus, as an offshoot of alligator hunting, that the roots of the Louisiana fur industry were laid down. Like the nutrias that followed, the muskrats were not initially welcomed. Trappers were mystified; New York fur dealers were not familiar with the small pelts. So efficient were the muskrats in eating up the grass on the cattle ranges that farmers in southwestern Louisiana offered a bounty of five cents per animal. Persistence, however, paved the way for acceptance. As larger numbers of skins were steadily reaped by trappers, a market was forced into existence, even though for many seasons the price hovered at around ten cents per pelt.

By 1940 a market for the Louisiana muskrat was well established, and the New York fur brokerage houses had recognized that its pelt was far more versatile than that of its larger relative in the north. It was healthier looking, the guard hairs glowed, and the color variations on each pelt were more exaggerated than those of the northern variety. A dark stripe runs down the center of the back, often giving way to golden-hued sides, and the soft fur of the belly is the color of cream. Furriers now marveled. By cutting the pelts according to color, they could produce undyed coats of great variation, some almost black, others golden, and still others cream-colored, plus all the shades in between. This was a boon in a business where subtlety of coloring can be crucial. An increase in demand brought an increase in the price to the trapper. After 1940, it hovered around one dollar per pelt—a big jump from the ten cents of a few years earlier. The 1945–46 season was the biggest Louisiana muskrat trappers ever experienced—over eight million skins sold for an average of $1.50 each. But the glory of that year was short-lived; during the succeeding years, nutrias began to chip away at the muskrat population.

Muskrat lodges had just begun to dot the marsh when Wilson Verrett was a boy. He grew up with respect for the little animals and learned to set his traps according to their feeding and tunneling habits. By the time nutrias began invading the marsh, Wilson's methods were established. Now, he continues to lay each of his traps with the same care as though only otters and muskrats inhabited the marsh. But he must work harder as a result. The heavy nutrias weigh down his pirogue, and the task of skinning them strains his hands. When he comes into the cabin after running the traps in his pirogue, his eyes have a deadness to them. He pours himself a demitasse from the graceful Cajun coffeepot that always sits on the stove and settles into his rocking chair. He sips glumly or draws on a cigarette. He stares out through the doorway of the cabin at the rippling marsh, his eyes still glazed, as if the marsh had won another round in the wrestling match he insists on perpetuating. Perhaps he realizes that his purist attitudes are getting the better of him. But then the old refrain begins: "Well, ah know one thing; I was borned usin' a pirogue, and ah'm gonna die usin' one."

When he gets up to go out and skin his animals, his shoulders are hunched over; his arthritis, which does not permit him to straighten his knees fully, gives him the pose of a heron about to take flight. On some cold winter nights, the arthritis creeps through his body, paralyzing his jaw and crippling his legs. "It's the charley-hosses," he says. "They come outta the night with the damp and ties me up so ah cain't move."

After an evening of Wilson's stories, silence fills the cabin, broken only by Tommy's whimpering as he dreams in his box on the floor. Azalea jerks upright from nodding off near the table. Wilson's lips delicately hold the stub of a cigarette; he angles his head toward the door as if he could see right through the heavy wood into the marsh outside. The conversation stealthily shifts from the triumphs of youth to the lonely dangers of old age. Crime has come to the marsh; cabin after cabin has been broken into; sometimes, with a numbing malice, doors have been smashed to splinters, windows shattered, interiors ruined. Wilson attributes it to "all that dope that makes people go crazy in the haid." He and Azalea live in constant fear that they will be the next victims. Though they know they are too old to defend themselves, Wilson still says, "Ah was borned in the marsh, an' ah'm gonna die in the marsh." Whenever an outboard comes up the canal, Wilson's and Azalea's glances slide past one another. Azalea furrows her forehead. Wilson straightens his back. The two of them go to a window, peer out from behind the curtains, and hope that the boat will not stop at the little wharf out there.

Five

Empires of Mud and Grass

Trappers once had the run of the marsh. When the boom in muskrat trapping had just begun, they traveled back and forth along the coast each season, according to where the animals were the thickest. Duck hunters were the only other people to use the marsh, and they just put up their blinds for a month each year, shot down waterfowl by the thousands, and were gone again. No one else paid any attention to the wasteland of muck, islets, coarse grasses, and directionless bayous.

But thousands of miles up the Mississippi, among the undulating hills of Illinois and Missouri and the tall-grass country of Iowa, farmers had heard stories of the Louisiana marsh. They had been told that its muck was rich with nutrients, that its grasses shot up to the sky, and that its waterways were muddy with sediment that had come straight off their farms. Each spring they had watched as the snows melted, the creeks and rivers rose, and the rich topsoil swirled away into the Mississippi. Some of the smaller farmers, left with fields of pebbles, dreamed of a paradise to the south where their soil lay mingled with the nutrients of half the country, soaking up the southern sun.

Some of these farmers followed that soil to its destination. Young men with a spirit of adventure, they weren't afraid of boarding up their houses, jumping on riverboats, and leaving everything they had ever known behind. They had great plans for buying up the marsh and repossessing their topsoil. They would drain away the water and plow the marsh grass under, and the land would produce crops once again. There was so much of it! All the farmland from the Adirondacks to the Rockies had been draining into the marsh over the centuries. There was enough land for hundreds of farms, and the young men who floated down the Mississippi had visions of grabbing it and selling off chunks to those who were sure to follow.

The state of Louisiana was only too glad to get rid of its wasteland, at a profit of even a few cents per acre. As the Yankee newcomers poked around the marsh, the southerners chuckled at their naïveté. As soon as they'd seen the alligators and felt the mosquitoes, in all likelihood, they'd board the first boat upriver.

One of these northerners, Edward Wisner, had grown up in the 1860s on a farm near the little town of Athens, Michigan. He wasn't like most farm boys. After graduating from the local high school, which was rare in the circumstances, he got a job teaching school. A few years later, he became principal of another school. Next he went to work for a bank, and after that for a newspaper. But during these years, his eye was always on the land. Like a number of others, he had seen how the spring flood waters carried the soil away toward the south.

Meanwhile, the occasional bouts of asthma that had troubled Wisner during his twenties had worsened until they were almost continual. Virtually a retired man before his thirtieth birthday, he received a strange bit of advice; his doctor told him to go south, where the humidity would relieve the condition.

Peculiar as the remedy sounded, it worked. Shortly after Wisner arrived in north-central Louisiana, his energy and ambition returned. His eyes sharpened, his face grew severe, and his lips were pressed together in a thin, firm line. Money and investments now became his religion. He traded his real estate for timber, and timber for cotton. Each transaction was handled by a bank he founded in the town of New Delhi. In the midst of his dealing, he decided to set up a town and name it Wisner, Louisiana. Today the town has several commercial streets and is on the Missouri–Pacific railroad line.

During these years of fortune building, Wisner never forgot the soil that had washed off his father's farm far to the north. He began reading books about how the Dutch had drained the Zuider Zee and how the Germans had reclaimed the North Sea marshes. The study of engineering techniques and soil chemistry filled his days. He moved to New Orleans and opened an office on Canal Street, the city's main thoroughfare. In 1902, he incorporated the Louisiana Meadows Company. Over the years, its investment in the marsh grew to a total of 1,350,000 acres—over a quarter of the entire area—for which Wisner paid from twelve and one-half cents to $7.50 per acre.

Once the initial purchase had been made, Wisner launched a fury of activity. Laborers by the hundreds were sent trudging through the marsh with shovels. They advanced in a phalanx, digging into the muck until they were half buried in it. After some of the water had drained off, horsedrawn dredges gouged out ditches in long lines across the marsh. Canals were dug and bordered by levees; dikes were put up to control the flow of water in and out of the marsh. Wisner oversaw it all—a master designer laying the groundwork for an empire.

But he campaigned on other fronts as well. He canvassed the Midwest, traveling by train from town to town, handing out flyers advertising his land, stumping the territory like a politician to acclaim the richest earth in America. Poor dirt farmers and entrepreneurs followed him back to Louisiana. Still others came by boat. In New Orleans, prospective buyers were greeted by the mayor, or sometimes by the governor of the state, and given the same kind of sales pitch that Florida real-estate developers give winter-weary northerners today. The price of reclaimed land ranged between fifty and one hundred dollars per acre; that of virgin marsh, between one and fifteen dollars.

Wisner's success was no small matter. He garnered fortune after fortune, and as soon as a new venture was completed, he bought a bit more the marsh. At one point he owned eleven land companies; if all the options they held had been exercised, Wisner would have been the outright proprietor of eleven parishes. Still ambitious to acquire more land, he went to Florida for a short time to dabble in the Everglades, with the same drainage schemes in mind. But he soon discovered that this part of the Florida coast was built upon far more obdurate foundations than the Louisiana marsh. Buried coral reefs frustrated the most persistent draglines. Having purchased 350,000 acres of the Everglades, he had to get rid of them. And it was in Wisner's nature to do so only at a profit. The buyer turned out to be Henry M. Flagler, another entrepreneur and gambler, a confidant of John D. Rockefeller. Flagler attempted to continue Wisner's scheme, but met with the same end. Wisner returned to Louisiana and Flagler to his penchant for buying up railroad lines on the verge of bankruptcy.

Wisner's activity in the Louisiana marsh stirred other Yankee entrepreneurs. They had seen the train stations of their towns fill with farmers and their luggage bound for Louisiana and a new start on Wisner's land. Though Wisner had a head start, the marsh was big; one man couldn't buy it all. New land companies were formed, under such names as Delacroix, St. Martin, Miami, Vermilion Bay, and Pan-American, and their representatives went south to stake their claims to whatever was left.

The appetite of the land companies was so insatiable that eventually not much of the marsh was left. All this worried one man who loved the marsh just for itself, not for its speculative possibilities. This was Mister Ned—Edward McIlhenny of Avery Island. As he saw the draglines working and the midwesterners filling the little towns on the fringes of the marsh, he set out to preserve parts of the wetlands. It was his intention to deed them to the state so that they could be maintained forever as wildfowl refuges. If the marsh had not been so expansive, there might have been a showdown with the land barons. But some corners still remained. McIlhenny decided upon a 13,000-acre tract on the edge of Vermilion Bay—solid enough so the Gulf would not overcome it, yet open enough so it would be attractive to multitudes of waterfowl.

Although McIlhenny was a wealthy man, he could not afford to continue the growing Tabasco business, keep up his luxuriant gardens, travel, and buy thousands of acres of marsh as well. He needed financial help. Members of the family had always been lucky before, and now so was Edward McIlhenny.

One day, as he gave his name to a clerk in a New Orleans sporting-goods store, a stranger nearby introduced himself. He was Charles Willis Ward of Chicago, and he had heard of McIlhenny's work with snowy egrets. The two men fell into conversation, and as a result Ward paid a visit to Avery Island, where McIlhenny opened his guest's eyes to the wonders of the marsh. To the proposal that he put up the money for the purchase McIlhenny had envisioned, Ward readily agreed. Today the area is in the hands of the Louisiana Wildlife and Fisheries Commission, as unspoiled as ever.

Encouraged, McIlhenny turned his attention toward a 76,000-acre marsh island just to the east of the original acquisition, and then to 86,000 acres at the edge of the Gulf. In each instance, a benefactor appeared—first the widow of Russell Sage and then the Rockefeller Foundation. As soon as the purchases were made, McIlhenny turned the territory over to the state. No land speculator ever touched it.

The farmers who bought from the land companies were in for a surprise. One by one, they began discovering that the marsh would not meekly submit to their plans for draining it. After the laborers had departed with their shovels from the ranks of ditches and levees of dried muck, the marsh came creeping back in the wake of storms and flooding. It simply would not dry out. And the soil was not as tractable as in the North. It had little staying power and easily washed away or turned acidic and could be revived only after mixing in tons of sand. Visions of a new American agricultural wonderland slowly dwindled as the marsh took back the reclaimed land as its own. Today, all that is left of the project is a scattering of rectangular ponds and lakes throughout the marsh—watery gravestones marking the locations of ruined fields.

The painful realization that the marsh would not lend itself to dreams of a lush, rolling prairie arrived before the land companies had sold off much of their holdings. Wisner himself was finally caught short, with hundreds of thousands of acres unsold. Only muskrats and other fur-bearing animals provided any income from the marsh. But now the region was no longer accessible to trappers. In some parts, those who had customarily set their traps found themselves turned away at gunpoint by company agents. The land barons intended to decide who would and would not trap the land. Even the chosen few, the traditionally hardworking and productive trappers, found the rules had changed. Not only were they now assigned to specific areas of the marsh; worse still, they had to pay the land company for the privilege of trapping, sometimes the exorbitant rate of 45 percent of the value of the skins they took. Nor were they any longer free to sell the skins wherever the price was highest. Every few weeks the company agents cruised the marsh by boat, steering with one hand and holding a rifle in the other—since as the paid hands of the land barons, they were not popular among the trappers. The agents stopped at each cabin, complimented the trapper if he had many skins, scolded him if he had few, but took all. They loaded the bundles onto their boats and brought them to be auctioned off to the highest bidder among the New Orleans brokers. On the next trip back into the marsh, the agents paid the trappers, but it was no secret that they skimmed something off the price.

Their employers, the land companies, also made money from furs. Indeed, some of the marsh, especially in Plaquemines Parish along the Mississippi River delta proper, was in high demand because of the abundance of fur-bearing mammals, a demand that increased with the popularity of fur coats in this country. Some individuals who had bought marsh parcels for farming and later abandoned them, repossessed their land as the price of furs rose. Yet, this source of income certainly did not compare to the visions held by most of the land companies. Plans for quick riches had been thoroughly squashed. The marsh was once again in disrepute.

Or was it? The presence of oil and gas along the Gulf Coast had long been verified; but no one had known what to do about it or been inclined to probe for the best way of extracting it. The country's first oil well began producing at Titusville, Pennsylvania, in 1859. It was soon followed by wells in California, but Louisiana remained very much an agricultural state, where little thought was given to modern technology. Had it not been for one man, the state's vast reservoirs of oil and gas might have gone untapped for years longer.

Anthony F. Lubich was a big bear of a man with broad shoulders, a large acquiline nose, and a flamboyantly drooping moustache. He was the kind of man who made the American dream come true, seeking riches with a hard stare, a shrug of the shoulders, and a wondrous single-mindedness. Austrian by birth and upbringing, he had not come to this country until his early twenties. In Austria, he had been a naval officer and held an advanced degree in engineering. In 1879 he traveled to Michigan to visit an uncle. The state was still on the frontier. Families were pushing into the wilderness, clearing fields, and building cabins. Lumbering was big business, and each little settlement had its own sawmill. In the town where Lubich's uncle lived, disaster struck when a sawblade broke in half and there was no replacement. The young foreigner stepped forth and told the worried townspeople he could make another one. He succeeded so admirably that he was asked to stay on and supervise the mill, a proposition to which he agreed. He applied for American citizenship, changed his name from Lubich to Lucas, and never went back to Austria.

But running a country sawmill was not enough for this man. He wanted to go west and explore. He spent a number of years trekking through the plains, then the Rockies, and then the West Coast, stopping every so often to prospect for gold. During these travels, he visited mines and talked to mining engineers about the newest techniques in shaft construction and flood control. Hearing that there was an opening for an engineer in a salt mine, he applied through the mail and was hired. So he arrived in Louisiana, where his assignment took him straight to Avery Island.

Lucas's job was to keep the mine dry, either by pumping it out or by preventing marsh water from seeping into it. That meant cruising about the circumference of the island looking for spots where water might penetrate. During these explorations Lucas noticed, as others had before him, a smell of gas in the air and oil that sometimes oozed out of the ground at the base of the island. This was nothing new. It had been known for centuries that salt, oil, and gas, sometimes along with sulfur and gypsum, come out of the ground in close proximity. It had once meant bad luck for a salt miner to strike oil. In 1829, salt miners along the Cumberland River in Kentucky had been devastated when torrents of crude oil spurted from a mine shaft and into the river. That had been the country's first gusher. But the miners hadn't known what to do with the gooey stuff floating in the river except to set fire to it. The river for miles downstream was transformed into a winding torch.

Eons ago, an inland sea covered much of what is today south Louisiana. Its eventual drying up left an accumulation of salt hundreds of feet thick. Today, geologists speak reverently of that layer as the Mother Salt Bed—and, indeed, it did give birth to the underground salt mountains of the Gulf Coast, as the result of an extraordinary process. Under the pressure of a load of sediment, tens of thousands of feet thick, that had been laid down by the Mississippi River's effluent, salt worked its way upward, pushing, ripping, and twisting in great shafts that wrenched aside the layers of sandstone and shale or simply bludgeoned their way to the surface, sometimes poking through to form projecting salt domes such as Avery Island.

Where the shafts had broken through layers of sandstone and shale, these were bent upward with their highest points adjacent to the salt. Water seeping into the lowest levels of these rocks filled up all its porosity so that the lighter gas and oil were forced to the top of the strata, next to the salt. There they lodged in great reservoirs, prevented by the density of the salt from any penetration, until they were unearthed by man.

Lucas's curiosity about mining processes was whetted by the obvious presence of oil and gas around the salt domes, but he could not think of a way of forcing a shaft through the semiliquid consistency of the marsh. On a trip to nearby Beaumont, Texas, however, the sight of a salt dome sitting high and dry in the middle of the prairie relieved his frustration. He immediately leased 27,000 acres surrounding the dome, which was named Spindletop. In late 1900, the drilling began.

Up until that time, oil wells had been drilled by cable rig, which operates on the same principle as a pile driver. A heavy iron-pointed wooden shaft attached to a cable was hauled up a derrick powered by horses or steam and then dropped to the ground again and again to break up earth and rock. Occasionally workers would scramble into the hole with buckets and picks to clear out the debris. Lucas began drilling this way, but at two hundred fifty feet he was confounded: He had struck a bed of quicksand. There was nothing to do but stand back and watch the stuff rise to the surface.

This obstacle, from which another man might have turned in despair, only made Lucas determined. He thrived on innovation; his greatest pleasure was to pull on his moustache and call up his engineering skill to break an impasse. The solution he came up with was one so obvious that it had eluded other oil prospectors: to use a rotary drill and barricade it from the quicksand by sinking an iron casing around the drill. Such a technique had been used only for drilling shallow water wells. It was expensive, and Lucas had all but exhausted his money. Turning to the nascent but already well endowed Standard Oil of New Jersey, he explained the high probability of finding oil around the salt domes of the Gulf Coast. The Standard Oil people scoffed. He showed them a few jars of oil he had drawn from salt leaks around the domes. They shook their heads and told him it was too heavy to refine.

After other oil companies had given him similar brush-offs, Lucas at last persuaded J. M. Guffey, a Pittsburgh businessman and partner of Andrew Mellon, to put up the money. Lucas rushed back to Texas and began to drill. Every day for two months, the bit probed deeper into the sandstone layers. Each night, it came up dry. The workmen

were discouraged, and even Lucas's spirit flagged. The well was now over a thousand feet deep and it seemed that it would probably go on getting deeper without anything to show for all the work and expense. But one day in early January 1901, as workmen climbed up the derrick to add another section of drill pipe, one of them looked down and was startled to see a stream of mud slithering out of the casing. A few seconds after they scrambled down, the entire casing and pipe began mysteriously to rise out of the ground. A minute went by, and then the well exploded; the top section of the pipe shot five hundred feet into the air; great blasts of gas followed and finally a geyser of oil. It was as though the earth's guts were being squeezed through a puncture in its outer crust. For the next ten days, until Lucas was able to devise a makeshift cap and control the flow, the Spindletop gusher continued shooting oil two hundred feet into the air. By now, a quagmire of oil-sodden prairie surrounded the derrick. A spark from a cigarette could have turned it into an inferno. Despite warnings that it might explode at any moment, tourists flocked to ogle the black wealth.

Within a few months, the land around Spindletop dome had sprouted a forest of derricks. By no means all of these struck oil. Even where the supply appeared to be plentiful, drilling in those days was a risky business. If you missed an oil trap by a mere few inches, the result was no better than if you had been miles away. But gamblers can be lucky, as the Heywood brothers were. The five of them—Alba, O. W., Clint, Dewey, and Scott—had grown up on the road, moving from town to town with their father's traveling theater troupe, setting up their little stage on village greens, and dredging up the lines for any number of plays out of their memories. Scott, the youngest brother and the most restless, left the troupe when he was in his twenties and headed for the Yukon to try his luck as a prospector. He did find gold, and as soon as he had worked his claim, he headed for home. But as he was shooting the rapids out of the Yukon, his canoe flipped over and every gram of the fortune he had made vanished into the cold water.

He drifted to California, where the talk had turned from gold to oil and where he heard one day about Lucas and the Spindletop gusher. He grabbed his hat, sent a telegram to his family, and headed for Texas. There, Scott's luck returned, and this time his brothers shared in it. They leased a hundred-acre section in Beaumont and twice struck oil, making a fortune with each strike. They now went into the real-estate business, buying up hundreds of acres which they proceeded to sell at $15,000 per acre. Life was good.

With oil pouring out of the ground in Texas, people across the border in Louisiana began to think they had been missing something. A group of businessmen at Jennings, not far from Avery Island, had seen oil seeping out of a rice field, and wondered whether there might be one of those gushers under the ground at Jennings. They went over to Beaumont and told Scott Heywood their story. Intrigued, he came back to Jennings with them, took a look at the rice field, and told them he would start drilling at once. The owner of the field, one Jules Clement, raised a temporary obstruction. He didn't understand what all the excitement was about and was afraid that an oil strike would ruin his rice crop—or that, at the very least, one of his cows might fall into the well. After Heywood assured him that even if both those things happened, he would be wealthy beyond his wildest dreams, Clement was ready to agree. The brothers began drilling in the summer of 1901. Their experience was similar to Lucas's a few months earlier. The drill went deeper and deeper with no results. It passed the fifteen-hundred-foot mark and still nothing. But then, with only ten feet remaining in the last section of drill pipe in the brothers' supply, the bit reached oil, and the fever struck in south Louisiana.

As in Texas, a rash of wildcat companies sprang up—the Spring Hill Oil Company, Pelican Oil and Pipeline, and the Prairie Mamou and Oil Mineral, to name a few. Derricks were erected overnight; fortunes in land were traded over bar counters; a few men got rich, and many others went home disillusioned. If the wildcatters had probed the marsh, the strikes would have been more numerous. But they stayed away from the mud, planting their wells on the dry ground to the north and west of the marsh. The young industry's technology had not caught up with the demands of the wetlands.

It was not until the 1920s that the oil industry could begin grappling for the riches that lay underneath the marsh grass. Then came the development of the wide-wheeled marsh buggy and of seismographic equipment that permitted geologists to churn over the marsh's fragile surface and plot the location of the salt shafts. Every square inch of the marsh suddenly came into demand. What little the land companies didn't already own, hopeful individuals now wrestled for.

One of the best known of the land companies that got their start during this time was the Louisiana Land and Exploration Company. A modern version of the enormous land companies that flourished around the turn of the century, LL&E, as it is commonly known in Louisiana, now owns 600,000 acres of marsh, extending from the Mississippi west to the Atchafalaya River. It rents out its rich fiefdom both to huge enterprises such as Texaco and to traditional fur trappers such as Wilson Verrett and James Daisy. People in south Louisiana generally have few good words to say in its behalf. Huey Long, in his tirades for the rights of the common man, referred to it as "that monster land company." Most of the ill will arises from its reputed methods of land acquisition—such as scavenging acreage once owned by poor people who fell behind on their mortgage payments.

But those acquisitions of land are minuscule compared with the chunk of marshland with which the company began—hundreds of thousands of acres from the estate of Edward Wisner himself, the original tycoon of the marsh. When Wisner died in 1915, he was a multimillionaire and owned 950,000 acres of marsh. Wisner's grandson, Richard A. Peneguy, told me this one day in his New Orleans

City Hall office. According to Peneguy, his grandfather left 53,000 acres, or so Wisner believed it to be, to four varied entities: the City of New Orleans, Charity Hospital at New Orleans, Tulane University, and the Salvation Army. The four beneficiaries were to share any income from the land, known in New Orleans government circles as the Edward Wisner Donation. A later resurveying discovered that the bequest actually amounted to 40,000 acres.

Everything else in the estate went to Wisner's widow and two daughters, one of whom is Peneguy's mother. The executors of the estate closed in like vultures, and within six months the three women were penniless and in danger of losing their last claim to the land. In desperation, the women turned to Henry Timken, an old friend of Wisner's and the founder of an Ohio ball-bearing firm. According to Peneguy, Timken offered to lend the estate half a million dollars, to be repaid in five years, so that the family's affairs could be straightened out. But Timken, says Peneguy, foreclosed on the loan before the period elapsed and, following a number of lawsuits, gained control of Wisner's land. But it was of no use to him; in 1926, he sold it to a group of investors who called themselves the Border Research Company. They were the forerunners of LL&E.

The Wisner family ended up with virtually nothing and might have remained that way had it not been for a Louisiana law which states that survivors must be able to benefit from the estate of a deceased relative. In 1929, the Wisner family sued the beneficiaries of the Edward Wisner Donation and was granted a settlement that gave it 40 percent of the income from the land, mostly from oil and natural gas royalties. Richard Peneguy is a member of the committee that administers the land—hence, his office in City Hall.

Like his grandfather, Peneguy dreams of land-development schemes, but to a much lesser extent. His dream focuses on 22,000 acres of the Edward Wisner Donation, a section of marsh opening onto the Gulf. He envisions it as one day being a gigantic resort complex of hotels, condominiums, golf courses, and marinas. For twenty-eight years, the dream has been a recurring one, and Peneguy, whose office brims with maps of the area, is baffled that the dream has not yet come true. "Everybody tells me what a great idea it is, but no one does anything about it."

He unfolds his lanky form from a swivel chair and fumbles through rolls of maps to show me what he has in mind for the development. As his finger traces over the maps, he says: "For all practical purposes, this area is just a sandbar with a little swamp here and there and a few raccoons and migratory birds. I don't make any bones about not being an environmentalist. I don't know the first thing about the biological value of marine estuaries."

He sits down again in his chair, folds his hands behind his head, and leans back, looking out of the window. "Yeah, I sure get a lot of lip service on this idea. I have to tell you I do a lot of dreaming."

Once oil had been discovered beneath the marsh in the 1920s, people no longer saw the marsh as a wasteland. It was just a hindrance to the search for the hidden wealth. Oil prospectors abused it. They dredged out canals wherever they pleased. Draglines lurched along, tearing great pieces out of the marsh; salt water surged through the ruler-straight troughs they left, filtering among the roots of the grasses and killing off many freshwater varieties. The channels served to flush water right out of the marsh, instead of permitting the runoff to follow a leisurely, meandering course down a bayou and to the Gulf, providing the vegetation with water and nutrients along the way. Now, its headlong passage tore chunks of peat away from the banks and gouged still wider channels. Parts of the marsh dried out. Willow trees took root where blankets of grass had grown, to be followed by shrubs and then by prairie grasses. Before long bulldozers were arriving to break up the new earth, converting it into soybean fields or subdivisions.

While the activities of the oil and land companies were drying out the marsh, the trappers prospered—not as in the old days when they had the run of it, but more than they had when the land was being sold to farmers. Oil changed the politics of the land companies. It also made them rich and fat. They no longer had to squeeze money out of the poor trappers' incomes. Nor was it in their interest to do so. It is one of capitalism's grand ironies that the land companies were now obliged to take paternalistic care of the trappers they had once bullied. The somewhat bewildered trappers became showpieces of public relations. Outsiders who did business with the oil companies now traveled the marsh. It would not do for these people, some of whom wielded influence back in New Orleans or Baton Rouge, to hear that the trappers were being mistreated. So the land companies did an about-face, reducing the cost of a trapping lease to

25 or 30 percent of the value of the pelts, and allowing trappers to sell wherever they could get the best price. The Louisiana Land and Exploration Company, now the biggest of them all, has gone still further. It no longer leases on a percentage basis, but charges trappers an annual fee, amounting in some instances to as little as one hundred dollars.

The coming of the oil industry eased the lives of trappers financially and provided them with some security, but it has tended to loosen family cohesion, once a powerful binding force in south Louisiana. The technological world guarantees a weekly paycheck and is thus an attraction to younger members of a family, who are not drawn to the marsh as strongly as their parents. Sons of the older trappers now work "seven and seven"—a week on a platform with the next week off. During the off week, the young men are back in the marsh, running their traplines—or, if they are like Wyndal and Randall Stelly, they leave their jobs during the trapping season and go back again after it is over.

Material changes as a result of the steady income are apparent everywhere. Suburban ranch-style brick houses mimic the sprawling flatness of the land they are built on. New cars—a new one every year—glisten in the driveways. Outboard motors get bigger; presents for the children become more extravagant.

For some people in south Louisiana, the changes have come too suddenly to be absorbed without shock. In the prairie town of Mamou, tragedy has been the result. Cotton used to blanket the surrounding fields like snow. When soybeans proved more lucrative, cottonpickers were put out of work. The older ones collect welfare; the younger ones drift away to the oil fields, severing family ties and upsetting the traditional balance between generations. When family life is shattered, some deal with the disruption by taking to the bottle; others commit suicide. An anthropologist told me that the suicide rate in Mamou exceeds that of any other town or city in the state.

Six

The Steadfastness of Cajuns

The origins of the population of south Louisiana are far more diverse than the landscape that has molded them into an identifiable unit. People came to Louisiana as several distinct ethnic groups, many of which remain intact. Most of the people in the little town of Delacroix, east of New Orleans, still speak Spanish. Many of the towns along the Mississippi south of New Orleans were settled by Slavs, who still dredge there for oysters. Germans by the thousands migrated to a bayou that the French accordingly named Bayou des Allemands. The Irish flocked to the banks of the Mississippi to build up the levees. Chinese immigrants who settled in the marsh and dried shrimps on platforms are said to have entered the country in an extraordinary way. Knowledge of their expertise in drying shrimps had traveled far by the 1870s, when shrimping in Louisiana was just becoming an industry; as a result the Chinese were soon in demand. American and European ship captains provided the passage from Canton to Louisiana, where many of the dryers sought refuge from serfdom. On arriving at the mouth of the Mississippi, the Chinese were stuffed into wooden kegs to avoid discovery by immigration authorities. Once safely isolated in the marsh, they were told by commercial fishermen that any who left their platform villages would be arrested and sent back to China.

Outnumbering all these other nationalities were the French. They came in several waves. The first, in the early 1700s, was made up of Breton and Norman peasants and of convicts and prostitutes from

Paris. Their numbers served as a buffer against British and Spanish encroachment. This wave was a slow-rolling one that did not come in with a rush. Gradually, these first settlers drifted out of New Orleans and moved up the banks of the Mississippi, where the land was parceled out in long, narrow strips just as it had been along the rivers in France.

A later, smaller wave of French immigrants came from an entirely different background. These were members of the French aristocracy who, made uneasy by developments that led to the French Revolution, had made their escape before the advent of the guillotine. When they began arriving in New Orleans during the 1780s, the French and Spanish residents who constituted the upper crust, and who had battled swamps, disease, and legal difficulties to acquire that status, were loath to share it with newcomers. How it came about that the wealthy refugees from Paris wove their way from New Orleans across the largely unexplored Atchafalaya Swamp to Bayou Teche is something of a mystery. But it was on the banks of the Teche that they chose to settle. And in all Louisiana, they could not have found a more beautiful place. The waters of the bayou are quiet, reflecting the live oaks that line its banks, and a dreamy mood prevails.

The French nobility created a wilderness playground along the western levee of the Teche—a formidable undertaking to have been achieved in such isolation. The main settlement in the area, St. Martinville, was known as "Petit Paris." The opera house attracted the best European performers. During the holidays, there were balls every night at which guests danced away the hours, garbed in fantastic costumes. Today, the town looks as though it has just awakened from a two-hundred-year sleep. Magnificent old buildings, crumbling but still upright, surround a live-oak-lined square; except for the huge trees, the square is all but deserted and the streets are lined with the now shabby remnants of the exiles in paradise.

Between the initial wave of peasants and the later one of aristocrats came the Acadians, the best known of the immigrants to Louisiana. The misery that overtook them during their wanderings after being expelled from Nova Scotia has been documented by historians and, less accurately, by Henry Wadsworth Longfellow in *Evangeline*. Their exodus was the frightful climax of two centuries of rivalry between the British and the French for control over North America.

The French had tried to plant a colony on Nova Scotia as early as the beginning of the seventeenth century. Severe winters, starvation, disease, and raids by the British had brought each effort to an end. But in the 1630s, a colony finally took root and prospered. Its members were peasants from the poorest French provinces, and they never had an easy time. The British were a constant threat, often a death-dealing one. Many of the Acadians were killed outright; others were captured and taken back to the colonies, where they were sold as slaves. The raids continued until 1713, when the French surrendered their grasp on Nova Scotia with the Treaty of Utrecht, and the British took over the rule of the French settlers. From then on the problem of the Acadians became still more serious. Regarded as untrustworthy by the British, who still feared the influence of the French in the New World, they were several times threatened with expulsion unless they swore allegiance to the British crown. The steadfast Acadians declared that they preferred expulsion to foreign allegiance—a resolve that is the more remarkable because France had never paid them much attention except as a foil to the British. The deterrent having failed, the mother country had quietly abandoned its offspring. Part of the reason is to be found in the Acadians' background. Unsophisticated peasants from Brittany, Normandy, and Touraine, they were hardworking, conservative, and very Catholic. These traits added up to a stubbornness for which the Acadians in Louisiana are still known.

Passive stubbornness can often make an opponent appear foolish. When the Acadians quietly acceded to their own expulsion, the British must first have been dumbfounded and then embarrassed. In what amounted to an acknowledgment of dependence upon the Acadians, the British now refused to let them leave. As tillers of the land, harvesters of crops, and builders of fortifications, the Acadians had become indispensable to the survival of the British troops. Moreover, they were on good terms with the Micmac and Malecite Indians, from whom the British feared attack if the peasants departed. There was yet another reason for not letting the Acadians go. During a century of settlement in Nova Scotia, they had become masters of the marshlands. They knew how to drain the marsh, how to build dikes, and how to control water levels. The British were afraid the Acadians would tear down the earthworks before leaving; they also recognized that few among their own ranks knew enough about maintaining the drainage system to ensure the growth of the food upon which all depended for survival.

The only way out of the dilemma was to try to populate Nova Scotia with British colonists. But time and recruiting were required before English farmers could be persuaded to leave their little hamlets for the often fogbound peninsula. By the 1750s, however, Nova Scotia was beginning to fill up with British peasants, and the land the Acadians had lived on for so long was needed to make room for the Britons. The time was ripe for the British to carry out their long-standing threat. Moreover, the antagonism between the French and the British was now reaching its climax in the French and Indian War. The thirteen thousand former French citizens in Nova Scotia would have to go.

Orders for expulsion came in 1755. Many Acadians escaped by fleeing into the Canadian wilderness. For thousands of others, a dreadful fate was in store. Longfellow may not have been far off in his description of the forced separation of families, the heartbreaking scenes on the beach, and the callousness of the British soldiers.

> *Wives were torn from their husbands, and mothers, too late, saw their children*
> *Left on the land, extending their arms, with wildest entreaties.*
> *So unto separate ships were Basil and Gabriel carried,*
> *While in despair on the shore Evangeline stood with her father.*

Most of the Acadians packed into the ships were transported to the thirteen colonies under a British plan for spreading them along the coast, so that they could never join forces and resettle Nova Scotia. Like most refugees, they were not well received. Some of the two thousand who landed in Boston were pressed into a servitude that was tantamount to slavery; any attempt to escape, they were told, would bring fines, imprisonment, or public flogging, since the colonists did not wish to have foreign ragamuffins wandering about their fields and forests. The Acadians who reached New York harbor were not even permitted to land, but were eventually deposited on the island of Santo Domingo. In Philadelphia, the reception was even crueler. The authorities there would neither let the exiles disembark nor permit the ships to leave the harbor. Smallpox broke out on board, and many died.

Connecticut and Maryland were the only colonies that accepted these people. In Maryland, the reason was a shared Catholic religion; today, one section of Baltimore is largely populated by the descendants of these Acadians. Other colonies grudgingly allowed the refugees ashore, but did not encourage them to remain. Some of the Acadians who were permitted to land began the trek westward over the Appalachians, bound for Louisiana, where at least French was spoken. Others ended up in such remote corners of the world as the Falkland Islands, the Leeward Islands of the Caribbean, and the jungle cities of Central America.

Even France now wanted nothing to do with its own flesh and blood. When British ships with over eight hundred Acadians aboard arrived there, they were waved away with the excuse that the passengers were now British subjects. The Acadians ended up in shantytowns outside Liverpool, Southampton, and Bristol, along with hundreds of others whom the authorities in Virginia had not permitted to land. After five years of a squalid existence, the Duke of Nivernois, a member of the French court, came to their rescue, or so it appeared. No sooner had he succeeded in bringing the Acadians back to their ancestral homeland, however, than he made known his intention to ship most of them to his estate on an island off the coast of Brittany, where they were to cultivate his fields as indentured servants. The French court denied him permission to carry out this scheme, and the wanderers were finally settled, some in Normandy and Brittany, and others further south along the Lot and Garonne rivers. They had come full circle, back to the same rural poverty their ancestors had left behind. But now they were looked upon as outsiders and were not welcome. Their accents, dress, and behavior were now different. Huddled together in small villages, they were ripe for exploitation. The Acadian problem had not been laid to rest.

Proposals for a solution abounded. One was to settle them in Les Landes, a deserted, sandy strip along the Atlantic coast. Another was to send them off to French Guinea. Whatever the scheme, the Acadians were regarded merely as a source of needed labor. In the 1780s, a pharmacist named Peyroux de la Coudrienne came up with a variation on this theme. He had spent seven years in Louisiana, which had been ceded to Spain at the close of the French and Indian War, and had won some favor with the Spanish administration. He had seen at first hand the continued need of the little colony for more laborers to

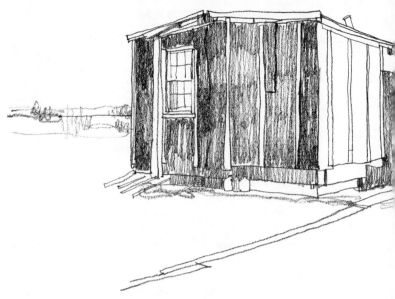

push back the thick forests and settle the bayous. The Spanish king, Charles III, accepted his proposal to bring in the Acadian refugees. So in 1785 seven shiploads of Acadians were brought to Louisiana, where by now many thousands of other Acadians had drifted from the thirteen colonies, the Caribbean islands, and elsewhere.

No diaries or memoirs of any of these refugees have ever been discovered. Although many were probably illiterate, there must have been some who preserved a written record. The only such account that purports to be at first hand describes the expulsion from Nova Scotia, a voyage to the Maryland colony, and a journey overland to Louisiana. It was handed down to Felix Voorhies, a judge at St. Martinville, by his grandmother, who had been told the tale by her grandparents. Voorhies published the story in 1907 under the title *Acadian Reminiscences*. The account is somewhat suspect, however, because it has less to say of the expulsion and the traveling conditions than of what Voorhies declared to be "the true story of Evangeline." Diverging from the Longfellow poem, it has Emilie Labich ("Evangeline") meeting Louis Arceneaux ("Gabriel") under the "Evangeline Oak," which still stands in St. Martinville, instead of in a Philadelphia hospital.

Another historical note was left behind by one Colonel Aubrey, the last French governor of Louisiana before the Spanish took over in

1763. So many Acadians were arriving in New Orleans, he reported, that he feared they might have to sleep in the streets, and he regarded it as his duty to find housing for the refugees and land for them to settle upon.

The Acadians were unusually well treated by both the French and the Spanish colonial administrators, for the reason that they could be made use of. During the 1760s there were only a few thousand Europeans in all Louisiana. Most of them lived in New Orleans. The rest of the territory—the forests, bayous, swamps, and marsh—was Indian country. As a buffer between New Orleans and that country, and especially as protection against attack by the Attakapas, the Acadians would serve nicely. Not only the colonists, but their Indian neighbors as well, dreaded the Attakapas. Alone among all the Indians of Louisiana, they were believed to be cannibals—a reputation that was no more than hearsay coupled with hysterical exaggeration. At any rate, the people of New Orleans slept better in the knowledge that Acadians lay between them and the Indians.

The first Acadian settlements were laid out close to New Orleans, wherever land was vacant along the Mississippi and its major distributaries. When the levees there had all been filled up, some of the Acadians struck out westward to the Spanish garrison against the Attakapas on Bayou Teche, the same area French aristocrats would settle several decades later. Meeting with no hostility there, the Acadian settlements spread farther west, into one of the richest as well as most inaccessible parts of Louisiana. Fertile prairies stretched to the north and west; to the south, the land was wet river bottom and marsh. The immigrants began farming the prairies and probing the marsh itself. They had large families and gathered into the tight enclaves that isolation and past oppression fostered. One such family was named Broussard. There are now hundreds of Broussards scattered about southwest Louisiana, all said to be its descendants. Today this part of the state is called Acadiana and most of its inhabitants are Cajuns—a lazy way of saying "Acadians," but one that is commonly accepted.

Cajuns have been the subject of a considerable literature. Most of it glamorizes their simple life style, their spicy cooking, their charming accents, their tradition of folk healing, and their seeming obsession with beer drinking, betting, and dancing. They are the pets of Louisiana, fondly portrayed with just a hint of ridicule. In New Orleans, where the Cajuns are cherished as nowhere else, people talk about their quaint ways as though they had not quite caught up to the twentieth century. Cajun storytellers circulate about the state, and their tales in dialect are endlessly repeated. An uninitiated listener to these fabrications tends to conjure up images of Cajuns as quite distinct in appearance and behavior from other white Louisianans, though in fact Cajuns are extraordinarily American in their looks. An exaggerated caricature of Cajun speech by comedian Howard Jacobs, published a few years ago in *Acadiana Profile,* a magazine about south Louisiana, reflects an all too prevalent view:

> Dey got a fallow wat eenlis' en de Air Corps, so dey put heem in wat dey call de parrotshoot deeveesion. He didn't like dat too much 'cause ary day, ary day, dey march to get tough to jomp out dem plane. Den de cap-tan make arybody come an' seet down, an' he say, "Ma friends, I want to 'splain you somet'ing. Wen you gonna got up dere you got two parrotshoots, wan lettle wan on de front wat open aromatically, an' a beeg wan on de back jus' in case dat leetle wan don' open. An wen you arrive on de groun', stay rat dere, 'cause it's got a fallow een a jeep wat's gonna come look fo' you. He gonna pass dere an' pick you op an' take you back to de base."

Ary day he 'splain dat to de cruits. Den ma frien' say, "Wan day we clim' een dat plane an' go way opstairs—maybe 8,000 or 10,000 feets. Den I jomp out an' wait fo' dat leetle parrotshoot to open aromatically, but eet don' open, so dat cap-tan musta jus' lie 'bout dat. Den I pull de ripcord on de beeg parrotshoot, an' eet don' open neider. Wat you t'ought 'bout dat? De cap-tan he lie 'bout de beeg parrotshoot, too. Me I bat you four dollar wen I got on de groun' dat jeep ain't gonna be dere eider."

This kind of humor has continued to affront the pride of people in Acadiana, especially of those who follow the traditional way of living off the land. Shunted from the start into isolated regions where they quietly worked the land, they have continued to live in relative isolation—largely by unconscious choice, since to leave the land and join the labor pool was a decision so jolting that many Cajuns did not even consider it. Their customs strengthened rather than diminished, although before the idea of ethnic revival came into fashion, Americans tended to make fun of anyone who was a little different.

That the Cajuns spoke French made them natural targets of ridicule as late as the 1950s. Most Cajuns over thirty years old have stories to tell of being punished at school simply for speaking French in the classroom. Randall Stelly still smarts from the times his knuckles were rapped by an angry teacher. Embarrassed even now to recall those times, he looks at the ground and paws it with his feet. "They hit ma hands good, them teachers, but I didn't know English good enough then. French was the only way I could of talked. But even now, I feel kind of, ya know, funny, speakin' French sometimes. It's like I was doin' somethin' wrong."

The stereotype of Cajuns as people who spend their time drinking beer and telling stories in a quaint accent has been just as damaging to Cajun cultural pride as the older ban against speaking French in the classroom. Many Cajuns thoroughly endorse the slogan, Laissez les Bon Temps Rouler (Let the Good Times Roll), as a means of survival. The Cajuns have now begun to transform mockery into a weapon of their own, in the spirit of ethnic revival. They boast about their beer drinking, fast driving, and quick fists. Some, with grins, refer to themselves as "coon-asses." Bumpers and rear windows are adorned with stickers declaring that Coon-Asses Make Better Lovers,

Coon-Asses Do It Anywhere, or Coon-Asses Eat Anything—Even Garbage, with a cartoon of a raccoon's rear, tail lifted.

Among the various theories purporting to explain the term "coon-ass," the most plausible dates from World War II, when French soldiers, amused by Cajun French, are supposed to have called those who spoke it *les connasses*. A slang reference to prostitutes, but also an affectionate term for back-country rubes, the epithet is presumed to have returned to Louisiana with the Cajuns and evolved there to "coon-ass."

Cajun culture is now unavoidably exposed to change. Even though parts of south Louisiana still belong to the timeless world of the marsh and bayous, other parts are in the forefront of development. At Lafayette, the capital of Acadiana, where the old business district has the square, solid look of onetime prosperity, but is now an empty shell, department stores, office buildings, and restaurants are to be found along the fingers of newly developed land that extend beyond the city. Shopping centers and subdivisions line the highways that have drained away the town's former vitality.

Despite the forces that have weakened the Cajun culture, remnants of it do survive. If Cajun institutions were all to die, the *fais do-do*—a children's expression that means "take a nap"—would be the last to go. The literal meaning notwithstanding, the fais do-do is an occasion for the dancing that is as important to traditional Cajun life as freedom of movement in the marsh. In the old days, families gathered en masse for weekend dances at someone's house, a different one each weekend. With telephones not yet common, word of the location of the next fais do-do traveled by mouth along the length of a bayou settlement. On that evening, when families had all congregated, their customary linear orientation along the bayou rolled up into a cluster, the children were put into a separate room and lulled to sleep by a quiet tune on a fiddle or accordion—hence, fais do-do. The dancing went on for hours, sometimes right through to the next morning, and it was an ordeal for the musicians. When they were totally exhausted, the signal that they could play no more was given by one of them, who went outside and fired a pistol in the air. The dancing was over until the next weekend.

Today, commercial dance halls, which are scattered throughout Acadiana, have become the scenes of the dances, and children stay at home in the care of baby-sitters. But the name fais do-do has remained. And so has the original function—a get-together for gossip and chat, an opportunity for the people of a community to keep an eye on each other and to sniff out any changes in the social climate. One Saturday afternoon when my wife and I were looking for a fais do-do to go to that night, it was Luis Romero who pointed us in the right direction. Luis owns a little store outside St. Martinville that he has turned, with a canny eye on Acadiana's nascent tourist trade, into a shop specializing in local lore and boudin, a spicy pork sausage that is as Cajun as a fais do-do. I bought some boudin and asked Luis if there was going to be fais do-do in a certain dance hall in Lafayette. He peered out of the shop window and exclaimed, "Mais, non, cher, tonight the fais do-do is at the Blue Moon in New Iberia. It's on Corinne Street. Anyone will tell you how to get there, tu comprends, non?" This was Cajun talk designed to charm a tourist. Luis was staring at me with the satisfied look of a country fellow savoring the good fortune that has placed him in the midst of a tourist bonanza.

In New Iberia, a town along the Teche whose main street is lined with colonnaded antebellum houses, the Blue Moon proved to be a sagging, ramshackle, one-story building on the wrong side of the railroad tracks. In this scuffed part of town, the trees are dust-laden, and the shoulders of the streets are likewise deep with the soft dry dust of the South. Between the scattered warehouses stand dejected shanties spattered with the mud thrown up by trucks during rainstorms. Ragged, big-eyed children stare from rotted porches.

Saturday night is *the* night at the Blue Moon. High school kids in 1955 Chevys roar back and forth in front of the hall, throwing beer cans out of the car windows. The air is so oppressively heavy and sullen that you can almost see it in the glare of the streetlights. Teenagers wearing football jerseys and the omnipresent baseball caps hang about the steps. Inside, a yellowish gloom is reflected from floor and walls. There are no windows and the ceiling is low. The red-covered tables surrounding the expanse of the dance floor are the only cheerful note, giving the place a jaunty air of expectation. Beer posters decorate the walls. We're All in This Together reads the message on one of them.

To one side, a bar runs the entire length of the hall. Bodies appear stacked against it, each equipped with a beer bottle. I envision the patrons turning as one, with piercing eyes toward the two of us. Elsewhere, except for a stage at the far end, where an accordionist is playing a few phrases and a fiddler strums idly, the place seems almost empty. Then, as my eyes adjust to the gloom, I see more people. Just under the stage, there are families seated at long tables—grandparents, parents, brothers, sisters, aunts, uncles, and cousins—a table for each family group. The tables are littered with beer cans, cups, packs of cigarettes, and overflowing ashtrays. In the midst of all this clutter, an aura of formal constraint nonetheless prevails. The music begins with a shriek of the fiddle and a din of foot stomping. Their faces serious, the men rise and approach their chosen partners. With a little bow, each holds out his hand and escorts his choice onto the floor. The solemnity around the tables is shattered into the rhythms of the dancing. Strutting adolescents in tight pants, with undulating buttocks, dance the three-step waltz with grandmothers in their seventies, the feet of both partners moving precisely in a pattern that has been drummed into their senses since childhood. Pot-bellied old men dance the Cajun two-step with their blossoming granddaughters, holding them close in a familial embrace, sidling past other couples with a quick wiggle of the hips and shoulders. Each time the music stops, the men escort their partners back to the family table and acknowledge the favor with another precise little bow.

Although the whine of accordions at a fais do-do still echoes through the streets of many towns in Acadiana every Friday and Saturday night, the dances are not the powerful community link they once were. Young people still go there to dance the Cajun two-step, but many more gravitate toward the bars and dance halls that feature Clifton Chenier, Doug Kershaw, or Rockin' Dopsie and the Twisters, whose music is built on a traditional Cajun foundation but with adornment from the blues or country-and-western. People lament the passing of Cajun country charm, as though it were the duty of Cajuns to preserve their ethnic purity so that the rest of us will have something besides ourselves to stare at for amusement. The loss of ethnicity comes down to much the same thing as the extinction of a species—one more layer of variety gone, one more reason to turn on the television and absorb its predigested fare. This would be well enough if a plastic monoculture brought happiness. But that it evidently does not do. Ethnic revival is on the upswing, but sometimes only when the culture in question has disappeared. Then the result is a fabrication of instant ethnicity.

The Cajuns are luckier than some others. Despite the blandishments of a shopping-center society, their culture is still alive at the core and is now undergoing a revival even before its own death. For this development, one man, James Domengeaux, is primarily responsible. Silver-maned and now in his seventies, long an institution in Louisiana's traditionally colorful politics, he is in some ways more powerful than during the 1940s when he was a U.S. congressman. In Acadiana, the word is that Governor Edwin Edwards catered to Domengeaux because he could deliver the vote of the French-speaking population. Domengeaux began his political career as a state legislator, and his rise to the higher office is partially attributable to the brashness he displayed in radio speeches against Huey Long. It is said that he was offered a job if he would shut up—which Domengeaux refused to do.

In 1948 he campaigned for the senate seat then held by the late Allen J. Ellender, but lost. The campaign had been full of southern temper and passion. The New Orleans *Times Picayune* quoted Domengeaux as having referred, in a debate with Ellender, to "the deafening roar of this wind machine." Having lost the election, Domengeaux returned to his law practice in Lafayette. After twenty years, during which he earned several fortunes serving the oil business, he looked around for an issue that would return him to the public eye. Most people in Acadiana had long been conscious of the deterioration of the French language. No one did anything about it. Domengeaux saw that the time had come to orchestrate a cultural revival. Years in politics and law had accumulated a stack of IOUs on Domengeaux's desk. He now put them to work, and the result was the state legislature's unanimous vote in 1968 to create the Council for Development of French in Louisiana.

Over one-quarter of the population of Louisiana still speaks some French, but not with much pride. The purpose of Domengeaux's CODOFIL is to revive pride in, and at the same time to give greater access to, the French language. When the organization began, the status of French in the state's elementary schools was dismal. There was not one certified French teacher in the entire system. Domengeaux alleviated the situation by importing hundreds of French teachers from France, Belgium, and Quebec; others from Switzerland; and even a few from Tunisia. He persuaded the state to print historical markers in French as well as English. In Lafayette the street signs are now in two languages, and stores throughout Acadiana display consciousness-raising propaganda posters with such slogans as Le Français à Present ou Jamais, Vive la Différence—La Louisiane Est Bilingue, Soyons Fiers de Parler Français, and L'homme Qui Parle Deux Langues Vaut Deux Hommes.

Domengeaux's law office in Lafayette is a mirror of the man, a lavish outer shell whose interior turmoil is no more than partly open to public view. The richly stained pine walls of his inner sanctum are hung with inscribed photographs of Presidents Roosevelt, Truman, and Johnson. The upholstery smells of wealth; curtains hang in rich folds; the carpet is a thick one, but littered with the papers that spill from an open attaché case like fruit from an inexhaustible horn of plenty.

On the desk at the center of the room, papers, books, legal pads, and newspapers are stacked in a jagged mountain range, behind which the diminutive Domengeaux leans back in a big leather-upholstered swivel chair. He wears an expensive-looking gray suit, livened by a silk tie that loops about his neck like an untucked ascot. This slovenly touch is in jarring contradiction to the silver hair of dignified length that sets off his ruddy face and to his smoothly throaty tone as he speaks into the mouthpiece of the telephone.

"Goddamit, she's always on the telephone or has some damn excuse or other. Tell her, please, honey, that I just have to talk to her. Will you tell her that?" There is no reason to doubt that Domengeaux has something urgent to discuss with the woman he has just commanded his secretary to get hold of. Wherever she is, I wonder if the force of that voice could reach her without the assistance of the telephone.

Domengeaux in performance is a master of studied distraction. He appears not to concentrate on anything for more than a few seconds. While I ask questions about CODOFIL, he is constantly swiveling in his big chair, leafing through one pile of papers and then another in search of a piece of information he never finds. Occasionally his eyes flit around the room and hover in the direction of the ceiling, as though the object of his search might have levitated there. He appears aware of my questions no more than to the extent of providing pat answers: "Ya see, the French is dying here and with it gone, our heritage is gone also."

But this air of distraction is a front. He is always ready for the next question and cocks his head as soon as I begin to ask it. The seeming preoccupation is a technique he has developed in his years of being interviewed. He is in fact waiting for the right question, one that will give him a chance to cut loose and expand on his passion for what he is doing.

When I ask him the reasons for the disappearance of French, his eyes suddenly light up and he plunges in with the uninhibited force of a pelican falling upon a school of fish. "We here are entirely responsible for the loss of the French language. We let ourselves be pushed around by teachers and school administrators until our children were forced to speak English and be ashamed of French. Those people are still suffering the psychological effects of that trauma. It did something to their spirit; it deadened it, and until CODOFIL came along, the heritage of this part of Louisiana was declining. We were joining the melting pot, just like a lot of places in this country."

His eyes sparkling, his body slides forward to the edge of his chair; he is sidling up to a passionate outburst, a demonstration of the southern temperament in action. It is wonderfully effective.

"When the legislators voted CODOFIL into being, I spent a lot of my time insulting those school people. They didn't like us because we were a threat to them. We were calling them to the carpet and instead of seeing us as a way of helping them provide a responsible education for our children, they thought we were going to embarrass them. Well, I guess we did, but that was only part of it. Now the gap between us and them is beginning to close. They're listening now."

He looks down at the carpet with brows furrowed, as if in deep study, then jerks his head upright to deliver a well-rehearsed inspiration. "Ya see," he begins, "we started out as the bastard of education; now, we're the illegitimate child; soon we'll be part of the family."

The telephone buzzes. "Yes, honey," he says automatically into the receiver. After a moment of listening, he turns to ask me, in a voice of silken politesse, if I would care to accompany him to City Hall, where a delegation of Belgians is about to be officially greeted.

"Ya see, we're trying to make our people here feel closer to their French heritage," Domengeaux quickly explains, as we walk over to the City Hall. "So what is happening as part of that process is that Lafayette is twinning itself to the Belgian city of Naumur. We went over there last year and now they're here. Next year, we'll have the final twinning celebration. Hey, monsieur."

The elderly black man to whom the greeting is directed gives Domengeaux a submissive grin.

"Ça va? Qu'est'ce que vous dites? Toute le monde ici parle Français, non?" The man smiles and replies something in French. Domengeaux is trying hard to show that French is the common language in the street. But his very American accent betrays the intended image. The man continues to smile and murmur incomprehensible phrases. In southern jest, Domengeaux berates him for not working harder, though—as he explains to the forever-smiling man—the fault is in his heritage.

Over fifty Belgians are waiting, clustered in the city council chambers, for Mayor Kenneth Bowen to arrive. The walls of the room are decorated with paintings of rural Cajun life. The artist, as though having taken Cajun culture to be indeed dead, had endeavored to bring the ghosts alive by painting them in day-glo orange, green, and yellow. The Belgians look as though they are at a birthday party for someone they don't know very well. They make an odd collection— dapper young men in tailored three-piece suits the likes of which Lafayette has probably never seen, slump-shouldered housewives with scraggly hair, dressed in ill-fitting polyester, a few elderly women with bandaged ankles, and baggy potato-faced men who appear to be farmers.

Mayor Bowen is a tall, broad-shouldered man with wide-set eyes and a big grin. The Belgians appear dwarfed beside him. Before presenting each one with a certificate as an honorary citizen of Lafayette, he makes a speech, predictably, on the subject of the cultural and linguistic heritage shared by the people in the room. The longer he speaks, the wider the gap between the two groups becomes, as French grammar and pronunciation both fail him. The Belgians look politely down at their toes. Finally, with a shrug of his big shoulders, the mayor turns to a French teacher from the local university and asks him to finish the speech. The other city officials who follow all give variations on the same theme, all apologizing for their "Français effroyant."

With the presentation of the certificates, the ceremony grows livelier. Much is made of the European custom of kissing on both cheeks. Mayor Bowen, regaining his savoir faire, waxes enthusiastic. "Oh, boy. This is the part I like," he exclaims, as the names of the

Belgian women are called. He gives the more youthful ones a peck on either cheek, sometimes murmuring for all to hear, "Ah, one more for the road." The Belgians smile broadly at these antics, with undoubted enjoyment, but also, perhaps, with wonder that Americans should display such embarrassment about kissing. In any event, there is no mention of the no less customary exchanging of kisses by European men.

In most of Acadiana's larger towns, the spirit of CODOFIL is clearly present. People talk about the idea and about Domengeaux's work with pride in their voices. They like the idea of foreigners coming to their corner of the world to see them revive their culture, even though what constitutes their French heritage may remain vague in the minds of many. Where all this has left the Cajun culture, which is only a part of the French heritage, is a question sober academics continue to probe.

The efforts of CODOFIL certainly can't have much positive meaning to people like the Stellys or most other fur trappers, crawfishermen, shrimpers, and sharecroppers. For these people, the French taught by the CODOFIL teachers amounts to a foreign language. Children come home from school spouting phrases and grammatical constructions their parents have never heard of. Even the idea of CODOFIL is remote. Conceived by the elite of Lafayette, it is administered by people who may never have set foot in the marsh. All this tends to impart one obvious message to the poor Cajun—that being a Cajun is still bad and that the French he speaks is not a language to be proud of.

Back in his office, Domengeaux swivels away from the question, his chair making a half-turn while his eyes comb the plaster on the ceiling. "What on earth is the point of learning a French that no one can understand outside of Acadiana? If you go up to Quebec and start speaking Cajun French, they won't know what you're talking about." Domengeaux is a practical man; his point is a valid one. But in assuming that with CODOFIL now established, everyone in Acadiana will follow its tenets, he is wrong. Though Cajun French may be dying, there are few Cajuns in the little bayou communities who are willing to learn another kind of French. It's much easier just to drop French altogether and speak English.

Given CODOFIL's strong hold in Acadiana, some aspects of French culture and the French language will probably thrive. And even though the project does not directly breathe life into the Cajun culture, a revival is still going forward, from the selling of boudin to the restoration of Cajun architecture. Nowhere is this more strongly evident than on Mardi Gras in the little town of Mamou. There, relief is to be found from poverty, the drinking problem, and the disruption of families with the loud celebrations that used to be typical of Mardi Gras throughout Acadiana.

The town has a pleasantly western appearance, with its false-fronted, two-story buildings. Horses ridden by boys are to be seen plodding along the main street in greater numbers than tractors; and on a hot summer afternoon, the place appears entirely given over to panting dogs and skittering chickens. On Mardi Gras the air of dust-coated somnolence gives way to something very different. Early in the morning, the street in front of the American Legion Hall begins to fill with costumed men on horseback. The twilight of predawn becomes an eerie stage where clowns perform acrobatics in their saddles, while werewolves skulk among the prancing hooves and the huge tractor wheels. Some of the men wear high dunce caps and paint their faces; some dress up as animals, and others as women. The "capitaine" and his aide always wear the costume—flowing purple and yellow capes.

A horn blares to signify the start of the "run," and cheers go up with a bellow. The horses are mounted and the procession heads out of town, followed by tractor-drawn flat wagons crowded with costumed figures who sway, gawk, and leer, unmistakably asserting that this day is their own. A beer truck joins the parade and so does a rickety wood-slat wagon with the Cajun band consisting of a washboard, a pair of spoons, a fiddle, and an accordion, whose musicians continuously play "La Danse de Mardi Gras." Those near the wagon join in singing the words that have been sung for centuries:

> *Capitaine, Capitaine, voyage ton flag.*
> *Allons se mettre dessus le chemin.*
> *Capitaine, Capitaine, voyage ton flag.*
> *Allons aller chez l'autre voisin.*

The "run," which continues for the entire day, is really a walk in a big loop around the town. Some years, it may be twenty miles long; others as many as forty miles. Whatever the distance, it is lubricated by gallons of beer and sustained on strings of boudin. At each driveway the capitaine brings his followers to a halt and goes to the door,

where he asks the owner to contribute a chicken for the communal gumbo pot that will be consumed in the evening, before the fais dodo. He waves his flag toward the costumed entourage, who gallop up the long driveway in a torrent of gleaming flanks, outlandish faces, and crazy hats that bob up and down. The beer truck and lurching music follow each stampede.

At most stops the farmer holds a squawking chicken in his hand—although frozen ones are beginning to appear—teases the riders a little, and then hurls the unfortunate bird into the air. The masked men rush with arms outstretched to intercept it, and as the chicken flutters down to earth, it is crushed and hurried to its destination by hundreds of scrambling bodies. The beer flows more freely with each released and recaptured chicken. Acknowledging the gift, the riders perform a drunken, whirling dance for the bemused farmer and his family while the musicians crazily bark out yet one more stanza in the endless song of Mardi Gras:

> *Les Mardi Gras vous remercient bien*
> *Pour votre bonne volonté.*
> *Les Mardi Gras vous remercient bien*
> *Pour votre bonne volonté.*

All through the day, they go from house to house, creating the sense of being other than of this world. The hypnotic rhythm of "La Danse de Mardi Gras" carries across the fields at the whim of the wind. Shouts rise and fall, arms are waved madly, and the whimsical flutter of the strange garb seems to have tumbled out of the seventeenth century en route to some crazy shrine.

Seven

The Land's Bequest

Cajun culture is in the midst of a revival, even though no one is quite sure what a Cajun is. Genealogists, linguists, historians, and anthropologists have tried for years to devise a recipe that leaves out no ingredient of the brew. The task is a thankless one, since history is always adding some new element to curdle the rest. The descendants of those who were exiled from Nova Scotia are obviously Acadians—i.e., Cajuns. But what about all the other south Louisianans whose language is partially or wholly French—the descendants of settlers who came directly from France, those from Spain, or those from Germany who proceeded to adopt French names? What ethnic slot can accommodate the offspring of the many mixed marriages—between Acadian and French, Acadian and German, Acadian and black? Domengeaux, the father of the Cajun revival, himself exemplifies the confusion. His paternal ancestors migrated from Bordeaux to Santo Domingo, where they raised sugarcane until they were driven from the Caribbean by followers of the rebel slave Toussaint L'Ouverture. His maternal ancestors, whose name was Mouton, straggled to Louisiana from Nova Scotia along with the true Acadians. Domengeaux doesn't know how to classify himself. Prudently, he leaves the issue open.

Most people in south Louisiana who consider themselves Cajun, are Cajun. There is no cultural membership committee to screen applicants and accept or reject them accordingly. The one real requisite is some knowledge of Cajun French. Names play a minor role. Paul

Tate and Revon Reed are the cultural leaders of Mamou. Their names are grounded in Anglo history, but they consider themselves Cajun at the core. Blood lines are more important than names. One group whose members *are* excluded from the definition are the Sabines—a generally derogatory term (but there is no other) for those few people who have a sprinkling of American Indian, black, and Chinese genes. Blacks are also ordinarily excluded, but that exclusion is by mutual agreement. Nevertheless, one black musician, Clifton Chenier, is sometimes billed as a Cajun, despite his color and even though his zydeco music is based more on blues than on traditional Cajun sound. Otherwise, blacks are referred to as colored people or more bluntly as niggers—a term that belongs unavoidably to the tradition and spirit of the South, where opinions are rampant and a swaggering vindictiveness is fuel for conversation. In Louisiana, identities are assigned with jarring offhandedness; diplomacy is to little purpose. A north Louisianan is a redneck Protestant, sure to be unfriendly; the southern third of the state is coon-ass country. The whole thing is as plain and simple as that.

A few years ago, Jon Gibson and Steven Del Sesto, two young anthropologists from the University of South Louisiana, came up with a definition for a Cajun that bypassed all previous historical and genealogical distinctions. They reiterated the traditional definition of an Acadian, but broke new ground to the extent of designating as Cajun anyone with certain crucial characteristics—close family ties, Catholicism, rural living, and the French language. The definition is at least easy and practical, and loosely reflects the present consensus of what a Cajun is.

One ingredient that always seems to be missing from lists people rattle off, however, is the Cajun environment. Certainly the marsh, swamps, and prairies do not affect all Cajuns in the same way. Yet the pervasive flatness of the land and the smell of the marsh are indispensable to the history of the people who live there. The character of the marsh has restricted the building of houses to a narrow strip of high ground alongside the bayous. The bayous, in turn, have limited the direction and the means of transportation. The seasons dictated employment and the food that went into a Cajun's belly. Floods could drive people from their shacks and droughts could force them to drink tainted water. Storms built up and broke over the marsh in a matter of minutes. Cajuns learned to live for the moment; and when the living was good, they worked hard and enjoyed life. When hardship struck, they clung to what they had, depended upon relatives and neighbors, prayed, and lit candles to Christ and the Virgin.

Life in the marsh is more predictable now, but its vulnerability is still immediate. All the conveniences in the world cannot halt storms. Marsh dwellers fear them as they fear a cottonmouth. There is not much that can be done about a storm that races across the marsh in minutes and leaves buildings and trees looking as though a steam roller had passed over. I felt that helplessness one night when I was staying at Wilson and Azalea Verrett's little camp. The day had ended with a flaming sunset and an ink-blue sky, but toward midnight the distant roar of a storm awakened us. The sound could have been made by nothing else; it was a front of noise rimming the whole southern horizon as it bore down on the little tar-paper shack. The marsh grass outside jerked back and forth as if in a futile effort to escape. In those suspended moments, the cruelty of the marsh was revealed as an absence of anything to cling to or anywhere to cower in. We had to face the rush of the storm with no more than strips of tar paper and slivers of cypress to protect us.

Wilson and Azalea paced back and forth in the glow of the kerosene lamp, murmuring worries and timid reassurances to themselves and each other. "Lord, Weelson, I scared, me."

"Mebbee she'll blow right over. We been through this before. She gonna veer off at the las' moment, you jus' wait," Wilson mumbled, his voice showing worry.

"I wished they would say somethin' 'bout it on the radio, but there's nothin' but that, what you call it, static." Azalea's voice broke, becoming a little squeal. "You know, Weelson had himself two brothers killed in storms. Down in the pass, they went over the side of the shrimp boats."

"Well, one thing's for sure; we're safer here than there. You bet ah wouldn't be out in a boat now, no sir."

Azalea began crossing herself. Outside, the roar was becoming deafening. The kerosene lamp began to flicker, throwing exaggerated reflections along the walls of the little cabin.

"If this storm gonna get real bad," Wilson said in a voice full of a fortitude that his nervous eyes belied, "what we gonna do is go into the fur shed an' lie down on the floor. She's solid, that shed. Ah put her pillings down good in the levee. But no camp can ..."

The storm stifled Wilson's words before they were quite formed. It hit with a great sigh, a momentary stillness as if it had concentrated all its energies on what was to come. Then, with a roaring whoosh, it bore down on the cabin, accompanied by the varying chorus of rain as it drummed on the roof. The beams ground against the pilings, and the walls groaned under the pummeling of the wind. Jets of air shot in between the planking and struck the old calendars right off the walls. Outside, the metallic sound of tumbling oil drums was throttled with painful abruptness, as if it were a murder being committed. We waited for the final tumultuous rending that would mean the dwelling was being lifted right off the marsh.

Tommy whimpered in his box, and Azalea ran over to him, cooing, "Oh, you little baby; com'on, be a big boy. We gonna be all right, us. You jus' wait an' see."

Two minutes later, the stars shone as the roar churned off to the northeast as impersonally as it had come. No lingering about this time to give Wilson's camp a few extra licks. The next day we learned that several camps to the north had literally vanished from their sites. The winds had reached a hundred miles an hour. The boards will be lying out there in the marsh for years to come.

Storms are the yardsticks of time in the marsh. Years don't mean much. The memories of older people focus about the 1915 hurricane. They may point to a hummock and recall that just before those winds struck a panther was killed among the palmettoes. Or if you ask a trapper when he built his camp, he may say it was "just before Betsy hit," rather than in the summer of 1965. Some people will blame the course of their fortunes on the changes brought by one storm; after the winds die down, the memory of them becomes the scapegoat. One trapper told me that he had not had a good trapping season since Hurricane Audrey ruined his corner of the marsh in 1957 and that his arthritis had been acting up since that time, too.

In the isolated reaches of south Louisiana, dependence upon others is a way of life. A silent fear based on uncertainty runs through Cajun culture. Some years the people have and some years they don't; on some days they have; on others they don't. In the old days, this uncertainty led to reciprocity. When a storm sank a shrimp boat, it was comforting to know that a relative down the bayou could provide you with oysters. The survival value of reciprocity long ago dwindled away in most parts of south Louisiana, as a result of stable incomes from the oil industry and relatively easy access to supermarkets, bank loans, and hospitals; but in the meantime it had been ingrained into the Cajun life style. Today the trait is called generosity and is one of the strongest influences exerted by the Cajun culture—a trait so easily imitated that newcomers to the region adopt it as standard behavior.

Giving is easy in the bayou country. It often doesn't cost a thing. The land and the water will certainly provide a few more oysters or crabs or ducks for a friend. In every bayou community, there is a continual exchange of goods from family to family in a never-ending chain of reciprocity—half a sack of crawfish for half a dozen cabbages; a dozen crabs for a couple of gallons of gasoline; and a turtle for a cooler full of catfish.

A few pockets of the marsh still exist where isolated people do in fact still depend on the reciprocity that was so important in traditional Cajun life. Ironically, these little enclaves are the ones inhabited not by Cajuns but by Sabines. Cajuns have traditionally disparaged Sabines, an ill-feeling that goes back to the days when the two groups were competing for the same rung of the Louisiana social ladder.

Blacks were on the same social plane as the Sabines, but the color made a difference. Whereas one knew blacks by the color of their skins, a Sabine might look just like any other white person, just like a Cajun. Now that Cajuns have pulled themselves up to an economic height unheard of thirty years ago, Sabines have been left to their tiny wet world, bordered by the marsh on all sides, governed by the whim of the weather and the bounty of the waters. As a result, Sabines now are often more Cajun, in the traditional sense, than the Cajuns themselves.

One of their communities is Grande Bayou Village. It is not marked on any map. It is not even incorporated. Two lines of shacks and small houses cling to the levees of Grande Bayou, whose route begins in the marsh and ends in the marsh, generally flowing parallel to the Mississippi. From the levees of the bayou one can look east and see, two miles away, the superstructures of the freighters and tankers as they glide past along the river. That sight across the marsh grass is a glimpse of the twentieth century from a foothold in the nineteenth. Over there, roads, telephones, supermarkets, and the lat-

est conveniences are taken for granted. Here, there is not even a demand for money. It is needed only for those sporadic trips to the outside—to the front, as it is called.

The only wheeled vehicle in the village is a little blue bus. Why it was ever barged to a place where there are no roads has long been forgotten. The marsh is gradually claiming it, as vegetation grabs at its rusting sides and the wet ground sucks at its bottom. The only means of transportation now, as in the past, is by boat. Most people own outboards, oyster luggers, or shrimp trawlers. The bayou is the link between house and house or between house and oyster reef. Perhaps in an effort to tie their community to modern ways, many of the inhabitants refer to the bayou as a "road," in announcements such as "I be goin' down the road to pass a spell with Ovide."

Some of the community's hundred-odd residents embody the picture-postcard, stereotypical Indian—bronzed skin, high cheekbones, and jet black hair. When these people push-pole a pirogue and the sun glints off their hair and cheeks, even the proximity of the cargo vessels on the Mississippi loses its meaning. Virtually all of Grande Bayou's people have some Indian blood, most of it Houma. When the French first began to explore the lower Mississippi Valley toward

the middle of the eighteenth century, the Houma Indians lived along the banks of the river in what are today north Louisiana and Mississippi. Generations of French influx and settlement uprooted them. Once, they had a settlement just south of Baton Rouge. The city got that name because the Houmas are said to have erected a red stick topped with a bear's head to mark one boundary between their hunting territory and that of the Bayou Goula Indians. As more and more whites settled along the river and its distributaries, the Houmas were pushed south. When they reached the levees of the bayous deep in the marsh, they could go no farther, and they have remained there ever since.

The strips of land they found were not in great demand. Indeed, so little used was the marsh that many outcasts took refuge in it. Escaped slaves concealed themselves in the maze of channels. The pirate Jean Lafitte is rumored to have used Grande Bayou as a means of escape into the marsh. Some members of his crew may have settled on the levees to raise crops and father children. Chinese shrimp dryers constructed stilt villages around their platforms, some of which were close to Grande Bayou.

Armand Dinette is the unofficial mayor of the little community of

Grande Bayou Village, probably because he is by far its most outgoing resident. He acts as its representative not only to officials of the land company that owns the surrounding marsh, but also to oil prospectors, barge captains and crews, and anyone else who happens to be traveling along the bayou and who passes his house on the levee. All such visitors tie up to Armand's wharf and spend some time sipping demitasses with him in his kitchen and complimenting his wife, Anita, on her fried shortbread. At each compliment, she shuffles her short, squat bulk—a figure that might just now have come out of the Sicilian countryside—toward the speaker, and with the faintest smile and lifting of her head, barks, "Wha'sa matter, you want more?" And then she turns to the stove and begins frying up another round.

Armand, with delicate fingers probing the air, speaks French with an intonation and grammatical construction that would astonish a Frenchman by its similarity to the language as spoken in Europe. The resemblance, plus his negroid features, indicate that his ancestors are West African. It is ironic that even though his Creole French is closer to the European standard than Cajun French, Cajuns have traditionally considered it an inferior dialect.

"I don't know where I learned to speak this kind of French. I've just always talked like this," he is fond of saying. "But you know what? I find that people have so, so much trouble with that Cajun French that when they hear me speak French, and I'm not boasting or nothing, they get so, so happy. They start smiling all over. I mean it."

Most people in Grande Bayou Village call Armand "Nonc"—a contraction of *mon oncle*—and Anita "Tante." She was born over seventy years ago in a hut surrounded by a little clump of oaks a few miles from the present village. She has left the bayou only five or six times in her entire life. Whenever she travels through the marsh now to help cull oysters or sort shrimps, she sits on a chair on the deck of the boat and clasps her hands in her lap. A dreamy, remembering look softens her face as she casts her eyes over the marsh grass. Occasionally she will point out a dead oak tree or an overgrown levee and share her memories with others: "See dat oak tree. I slept under it before the 1938 storm when it was kilt. My daddy and me had been hunting turtles and got caught in the dark."

Armand is not a native of Grande Bayou. He was raised on the banks of the nearby Mississippi, but when he was a young man he came to the village to live with his sister. He met Anita's father before he met Anita herself. One day, unbeknownst to one another, both of them were hunting in the same part of the marsh—Armand on a levee and the older man from a pirogue. Anita's father was a magnificent looking man. In a portrait of him and her mother that hangs in the house on the bayou, he looks somewhat like an archetypical Indian chief, perhaps a relative of Sitting Bull. It was an image he was apparently proud of. When Armand saw the man poling his pirogue toward him, he tried to hide. "I didn't know what to do. I didn't know nobody around here then and here comes this wild Indian down the bayou, heading straight for me. I went right around this palmetto and hoped he was going to pass me by. But you know what he did? The closer he came to where I was, the faster he was polin' until he got to the bank an' jumped right out an' started to run up the levee right at me. Oh, was I scared. I said to myself, 'Lord, no one told me that they still got wild Indians 'round here. I'm gonna die for sure.' An' then you know what happened? He got up to the palmetto an' pushed it aside and looked down at me on the ground, an' you know what, he burst out laughing like he was going to die. I thought he was never gonna stop. He was always trying to scare people into thinkin' he was the last wild Indian."

The older man befriended Armand and introduced him to his daughter, Anita. Single people of marriageable age have always had a hard time finding partners in the community. Now they mostly just move away and seek a mate elsewhere, but in those days they stayed and hoped. When a potential spouse appeared, families pounced, especially those of the young women. Anita's family opened its arms to Armand, fed him, entertained him, and courted him. That he was already married made little difference, for in the world of the marsh accommodations can be made to circumvent whatever is inconvenient. Armand wanted to divorce his wife, but did not have enough money to hire a lawyer. He and Anita just began living together, or "took up" as Armand says. That was thirty-three years back; three years ago, he finally got the divorce and he and Anita were married.

Armand showed me the bayou where Anita's father had set the relationship in motion. We were out in the marsh with Armand's outboard, checking his pumpkin and squash crop. Each spring, wherever he finds a spot of high ground, Armand cuts away the vegetation to expose the black earth and plants a few seeds. Now the vines had spread all over the levees, their route through the long grass marked by streamers of yellow blossoms.

"When them pumpkins get big, I'll give them to people along the bayou. You know, I like to give things. Everyone here does that. Now, I don't trawl for shrimp no more, but I sure like shrimp. So I give someone some pumpkins. Later, when the shrimp are running, he give me some shrimp.

"Now, we gotta go real quiet here 'cause that bayou is full of 'gators and they scare easy." We were ascending the side of the levee, and as we neared the top we crouched down and peeped over. An eight-foot alligator lay sunning itself on the opposite levee. Five or six more hung in the water, only their eyes and snouts visible. After several minutes another alligator rose in their midst—first the eyes, then the nostrils, and finally half the length of its back. Armand began fidgeting next to me. Finally, he could control himself no longer. "Do you see that 'gator. He must be fo'teen feet long," he told me in a grating whisper. "I haven't seen anything so big in twenty-five years. Why, if I was still polin' I'd find out where his den is." Suddenly, the bayou before us was empty and on the opposite levee there was only bare earth. The surface of the water remained calm; not a ripple disturbed it. "Isn't that something!" Armand shouted with joy. "Isn't that something to know that we got a back-yard full of pumpkins and alligators."

What is most remarkable about Grande Bayou is that the pace of life there is almost undiscernible. Except in the trapping season, which is tied to the cash economy, day-to-day life goes on in whatever fashion the village's inhabitants choose. True, some of the more ambitious people start out for their oyster reefs early in the morning, and during the shrimp season the bayou is crowded with boats; but in general, food is gathered only as it is needed. It is easy to come by. During low tide, the exposed banks of the bayou are lined with oysters. One sweep of a trawl might produce twenty pounds of shrimps; a shrimp on a hook will bring in a sea trout or redfish; and a trap baited with fish entrails will fill with crabs in no time.

The only scheduled events are the twice-daily passing of the schoolboat, to pick up the children from the wharves in front of their homes in the morning and return them in the afternoon. As the boat travels up and down the bayou, children's voices sound over the water. But between trips, the community nestles into the marsh as quietly as the rest of the marsh's indigenous life. The school was built recently, in a canal tucked off the bayou. Gleaming white under the hot sun, it is by far the newest structure in the settlement and is the pride of the inhabitants.

The only other event one could tell time by is Sunday morning, when people get into their boats and head down the "road" to the Presbyterian church halfway down the bayou. It is a low, long building with a stubby, dunce-cap-shaped steeple. Directly across from it on the other side of the bayou, and surrounded by a neat white picket fence, is the cemetery. That the deceased cross the water on their last journey before they are laid to rest is fitting, since the bayou is the lifeline of the village, serving its every need.

Armand and Anita are faithful adherents of the church. Armand is a newcomer. He used to be Catholic, until one day when a Presbyterian missionary began talking to him about religion. "He was a fine, fine man," Armand told me, "and he talked to me real sincere. And I remember that after he talked to me for a good while, he said something to me that I'm never goin' to forget. It was so, so strong. You know what he said? He said that anyone who gets down on his knees before anyone but God is sinning. And then he asked me if I went to confession. I told him, 'Sure, of course, I go to confession,' an' he asked me if I kneeled before the priest when I confessed, an' I told him that I did, and then he kind of looked at me long and slow and he said real soft, 'Well, then, you have been sinning all these years.'"

Armand sat for a moment shaking his head. Both hands gripped the arms of the chair he sat in, and he stared at the floor between his feet.

"Lord, I sinned something terrible those days. And do you know, after that missionary told me that, I joined the Presbyterian church right down there. I have felt so good and clean ever since."

Despite the solemn tranquillity of the community at large, the rocking chairs in the old couple's house are usually filled with gossiping women and men in earnest conversation about the price of skins and the numbers of shrimps. There are also children flitting from one adult to another in an endless quest for attention—which they invariably receive with a caress and sometimes with a cookie. Three regulars are Margie and Doris Sylve and their six-year-old son, Scott. Margie's real name is Homer, but no one calls him anything but Margie. He is a big man, with features of the same sort as Anita's father, except that his graying hair is frizzy. He comes in three or four times a day, plunks down for a demitasse, and rocks back and forth. No one expects much from him in the way of conversation. He is accepted for his open, unquestioning face and his habit of giving. Each time he enters the house, he leaves something outside the door. It may be a few dozen oysters, a dozen crabs, or a few pounds of shrimps. He never announces his offering, and Armand never acknowledges it.

Much of the giving has to do with Scott. Up and down the bayou, he is an adored child—perhaps because, like his father, he has such an open honesty about him. Doris makes no excuses about spoiling her youngest son. "He is the most adorable child I ever see. Why, I wouldn't sell that child for a hundred dollar," she says, throwing back her head with a laugh.

Where Margie is silent, Doris is full of talk. "You know what," she said to me one day as she sat with Scott perched on her lap, pulling gently at the curls that cover his head. "When this here child was born, everybody up and down the bayou wanted him. They said, 'Oh, my, he's so cute, I want to raise him up in my house.' But I wouldn't let them, not this one. He was my little jewel. Nonc and Tante are the only ones beside me that are going to grow you up."

In bayou communities, children are sometimes cast about like seeds. In their enviable state as recipients of community-wide love and fondling, they are usually raised by a number of families, often on an informal basis but occasionally by formal arrangement. Armand and Anita, who never had any children, raised as their own daughter a girl whose parents live only a few hundred yards down the bayou. Now grown, she has moved away from the community, but returns from time to time to visit her two sets of parents.

Doris and Margie are probably among the poorest people on the bayou. Their only source of income is through fur trapping. Everything they eat comes from the marsh. When Scott was born, they already had three other children to raise. Recognizing the situation, many people along the bayou offered to take him, but Doris would have none of it. The dilemma resolved itself when Nonc and Tante agreed to feed and informally parent Scott. But he still lives in his natural parents' house.

The remarkable give-and-take of people in isolated bayou communities is a somewhat poetic reflection of the whole economic structure the environment has molded. Life is lived from season to season.

Some seasons produce food, some desperation. Within this irregular cycle, possessiveness would be a dooming restriction. What belongs to Armand also belongs to Margie, and vice versa. Not many communities now adhere to this once generally accepted means of survival. But Grande Bayou is not like most communities; it has not yet caught up to the present. Tradition-oriented Cajuns would be proud to see it—if its inhabitants were not Sabines. And that, of course, is just the reason it still exists, even though it is showing the first signs of eventual death throes. It is dying not so much because its young people are moving away but because those who live on the outside want a slice of the calm the marsh offers. They are building weekend camps on either end of the village, and during summer weekends they roar around the bayou in their outboards. The state has plans to build a road into the village. Electricity was put in a few years ago, and telephone wires are soon to be strung across the marsh. Given all that modernization, Grande Bayou will catch up fast.

Eight

Dance of the Oyster Luggers

Jim Daisy begins each new venture with a crescent moon. As soon as the trapping season ends in late February, he returns to his beloved occupation, oystering—but not until the moon is fresh. Several years ago, he had to wait two weeks in addition to a Monday that began on the thirteenth, a bad-luck day in Jim's experience, for this to happen. The wait cost him several thousand dollars in undredged oysters. That didn't bother Jim. Tradition has irrevocably taught him to mind the dictates of superstition.

On the eve of Jim's oystering season in 1978, the spring's first hot day was just being nudged aside by a cold front. Willow trees were bursting into a haze of green, and water hyacinths had already given parts of Bayou du Large's surface the crispness of lettuce. The community along its banks, where Jim lives when he is not trapping, was settling into the patchwork arrangement of business and sloth typical of the summer months. Children ran back and forth across the road, dogs with foolish expressions trotting behind them. Half-built shrimp boats squatted on oil-drum rollers in front yards where men stood around in casual conversation.

In Jim's house, the tension ran high. Excited members of the family spilled out through the front door, across the road to the edge of the bayou where the three oyster luggers were moored, and then back to the house again with supplies, orders, questions, and gossip, all in an effort to dispel the cooped-up feeling of a winter spent with too many muskrats. Jim's lips were pursed and his wide eyes jerked about, intense with preoccupation. As darkness fell, the excitement was confined to the kitchen of his house. The men clustered around the table, smoking cigarettes, talking oysters, and watching young children crawl around the feet of Rachel and Sheena, Jim's two daughters, who were frying up a bunch of shrimps and soft-shell crabs. A boy ran around the table, stopping every so often to blurt out how many oysters he could eat. Sheena, an adolescent bundle of flirtation, sidled up to her father with a page of newspaper ads and pointed out the several kinds of clocks, radios, and clothes he might buy her. Jim made an effort to examine each item, but his fingers drummed distractedly on the table and his eyes jumped about, looking first at Willie, then at his brother Buddy, and finally at Shorty, a blond trailer-truck driver who hauls oysters from Bayou du Large to Pensacola, Florida.

"Yuh know what I'm worried about," Jim said to no one in particular. "I'm worried about this cold front. It's gonna make us some thick fog in the mornin'. An', you know, I'm jus' not sure that we can git down the bayou in that kind of fog. That's what I'm worried about."

"Yup," replied Buddy, an oysterman himself who shares an eight-hundred-acre oyster lease with his brother. "That fog is really rollin' in. You won't be able to see from here to the bayou tomorrow."

Jim snatched his pack of cigarettes off the table and took out one, rolling it a moment between thumb and forefinger before reaching for his lighter. "They say they got some nice salt in 'em now," he said in a light voice, as though trying to change the tone of the gathering. "Man, there's nothin' like a salty oyster. The water's gotta be jus' right."

He stroked his chin for a moment. "I sure do hope it don' rain up further. That fresh water on the reef will ruin the taste."

"Well, I do buhlieve we got to get us some rain," Willie drawled out. "You ever heared of spring when they don't get rain?"

"I tell you, they got some rain over in Florida," Shorty put in. "When I left this morning, I could scarcely see anything. I floated halfway over here, I swear." He leaned back in his chair and stuffed his hands into his trouser pockets, waiting for a response. Shorty drives over from Florida three times a week, and each time he spends the day along the bayou, driving from lugger to lugger to buy oysters. The local people hold him somewhat in awe, not only for his big truck, but also for the distance he covers. To most people along Bayou du Large, Florida is so far away it's just a name.

No response was forthcoming. Jim jumped up and paced once around the table. "Com'on," he said with a note of irritation and a wave of his hand. "We're gonna watch television. Com'on, let's go an' set in the livin' room. They got some shows on the television." Jim's nerves were frazzled, and he perhaps assumed that everyone else was in the same condition. All would be put right by the television—the instant tranquilizer.

The house on Bayou du Large is a far cry from Jim's cabin on Buckskin Bayou. It is a compact modern structure covered in wide clapboards, with a carport in front. When all the Daisy vehicles—Jim's pickup truck and his big car and the new one belonging to Dwight—are parked in the carport, the house is almost hidden from view. Its kitchen contains conveniences such as the marsh cabins have never seen; gadgetry overflows the drawers and cupboards. Elaborate dresser sets crowd the bedrooms. The walls are thick with colorful prints and gleaming ceramics. But the living room outdoes the rest of the house. Red and black are the predominant colors. In the bayou country, such contrasts are startling. The black of the shiny Naugahyde-covered armchairs and sofa draws occupants like matter toward a black hole. Once seduced, they sink in with a squishing sound that ends in a sigh. Feet become ensnared in a wilderness of brilliant red shag. Red satin wallpaper envelops the room in a mesmerizing sheen. In one corner a sturdy color television console looms like a citadel.

On this particular evening it was blasting forth the exuberant whimsy of Sha Na Na. As one of the group did a satirical imitation of Chubby Checker, the viewers settled down into throaty chuckles and then into silence. While Willie fell fast asleep and Dwight lay motionless on the shag carpeting, Buddy and Shorty stared transfixedly at the screen. Sheena and Rachel hung in the doorway, their eyes shifting from television to stove and back again. The tranquilizer had taken effect on everyone but Jim, who restlessly massaged his chin, rubbed his eyes, smoked cigarettes, and thought about oysters.

In the warm waters of Louisiana's brackish estuaries, oysters grow at a prodigious rate and account for almost half this country's annual production. They can reach market size—a length of three inches—in five months, although the average time is two years. In the beds along the Chesapeake Bay or off Long Island, the other two major growing areas of *Crassostrea virginica* Gmelin, four years is the average. Although Jim's love of oysters often launches him into conversational ecstasy, he will not eat one from the beginning of April to the beginning of October. No self-respecting oysterman will.

"I jus' don' like the thought of it, you know what I mean," says Jim with a grimace. "It's all that milk in there. They say they taste jus' the same, but I never et a milky oyster. There's jus' somethin' wrong about it."

"If you ask me," says Willie, "I think jus' the sight of a milky oyster changes the taste of it. It's like eatin' a white hamburger. Who'd want to eat one of them? That's why they got to wash those milky oysters. They take 'em to the processing plants and wash 'em over and over until the milk's all gone. By the time they finish, there's nothin' left that ever tasted much like an oyster."

The "milk," the only breeding color the understated oyster displays, is produced in the female by the eggs and in the male by the sperm. With the warming of the waters in the spring, the eggs and sperm are released, and if all goes well they collide—a less haphazard business than it might seem, since oysters live virtually glued to one another; the water immediately surrounding their reefs may turn hazy with sperm and eggs. Within hours after the meeting of the two, a larva forms and swims about with the aid of hundreds of cilia that wave about like oars gone awry. An oyster's ability to move freely lasts from two to four weeks. After that, the weight of its growing shell drags it to the bottom, where it will remain cemented to rock, old shell, or another oyster for the rest of its life, all the while pumping water in and out at a rate of three gallons an hour as it grows. And several times a year, it releases sperm or eggs. The chances are very good that an oyster will be able to do both during its lifetime. *Crassostrea virginica* Gmelin has the peculiar ability of performing either as a male or a female, but never as a hermaphrodite, a trait reserved for some other mollusk species. In Louisiana, as along the eastern seaboard, most oysters begin their reproductive lives as males. By the time they spawn a second time, enough of them have changed to females so that a given reef will have a fifty-fifty sexual ratio. In later life, oysters tend towards femaleness and the larger inhabitants of a reef will probably be female.

At daybreak, Jim's oyster luggers—the *Jerrie Allen,* the *Clayton,* and a nameless smaller boat of hybrid design—crept in single file down Bayou du Large. Only ghosts of the community's ordinary life were

visible through the whiteness. Corners of buildings, telephone poles, moored shrimp boats, and occasional parked vehicles slid into view and disappeared like things half remembered. Branches of dead cypress trees, naked but for hanging snarls of Spanish moss, reached down out of the white opacity to grapple for the boats. The silence was chilling. Not until the luggers reached Lake Mechant did the sun break through, tearing at the fog to reveal a flat expanse of muddy and sullen water whose far shores hid below the horizon. In this calm solitude, the three small boats were no more than toys steaming across a vast bathtub. They could almost have been miniature replicas of the Mississippi River steamboats of a century ago, minus the twin smokestacks and the paddle wheels. The *Clayton* was a classic craft. She fairly danced on the water, her round-bottomed fifty-foot hull supporting an overhanging deck upturned fore and aft to give her a deceptively light appearance considering her ample beam. Her foredeck was roofed with canvas stretched tight and flat over a pipe framework. Rounded about the bow, it gave the boat an airy outline. A little semicircular cabin with portholes and windows rose from the stern, and a cockeyed stack above the roof bespoke a welcoming warmth. Amidships, the gunwales had been built up with a latticework of freshly painted white boards to prevent the oyster sacks from falling overboard. The latticework and the awning are the identifying marks of any Gulf oyster lugger.

Luggers dredging for oysters present an even lovelier sight. When we reached Buckskin Bayou, opposite Jim's cabin, they began a kind of dance, circling lazily over the reef in an intricate series of movements of which family tradition, competition, the boats' design, and the abundance or scarcity of oysters are all a part. Each lugger carries a captain and a crew of two. The Daisy men were the captains, and their cousins and nephews from along the bayou made up the crew. They were far hungrier for a job in the marsh than for one that would take them out to the oil platforms, even though the pay on the marsh was poor—a dollar a sack—and they had to work fifteen or sixteen hours a day. During that time, if they were lucky, they might make forty or fifty dollars.

As the futures of sons revolve about the lives of fathers, so Willie and Dwight circled their luggers around the *Jerrie Allen* with Jim at the helm. The *Jerrie Allen* was the focal point; the two other luggers responded to her movements as though connected to her by a gossamer cord. Dredges scraped the oysters from the bottom as she circled up and down the bayou. At times the other two boats passed within twenty feet of her, and at others, they were a hundred or more yards distant; but there was no doubt that the movements of all three boats were connected. If their courses had been etched into the bayou's surface, the design woud have been a mesh of interwoven circles.

When any two of the luggers approached one another, just barely avoiding a collision, the crews would exchange a fierce banter grounded in competition, hard work, and the hope for just one more sack of oysters. Back and forth it went, at first a tumble of shouted gibberish above the creak of the dredges, dying away as the boats drew apart, and then shutting off as abruptly as a spigot.

"Here they come aroun' agin."

"They don' look like they doin' much work."

"Look it Black Boy there. He look like he was jus' out for an afternoon with one of them sports."

"Hey, listen to all that talk comin' our way. I buhlieve they got a whole ocean liner of people over there. They talkin' so much they gonna scare the oysters."

"How many sacks ya got?"

"We got six an' we're goin' on sixteen. We're not lettin' down Uncle Jim."

"Well, you talk so much, you don't have the time to do any dredgin'."

"We so good at this, we could go huntin' alligators and still git more sacks than you'll ever git."

"We'll be out here till midnight; an' then see how many sacks we got?"

"You stay out here that late an' yer ole lady'll run off with someone, y'hear."

"Hey, while you're settin' there yellin', we jus' got us two more sacks."

"Yeah, but now you is pooped out an' we're all rested up."

"Next time 'round, you keep yer eyes on us an' we'll show you how to dredge some oysters."

And so on and so on, each exchange grating on a few more nerves and producing a few more sacks.

On the deck of each lugger, the dance set into motion by the dredging was precise, repetitive, and exhausting. It was choreographed to the groan of the winches and the thud of oysters tumbling onto the decks. Oyster luggers have two wheels to steer by, one in the cabin and the other just aft of the bow. At the forward wheel, the captain reigns over a tiny domain—two rusting dredges and a work space no larger than a Ping-Pong table. His winch controls are within easy reach, but his movements as one dredge is dropped and the other is raised are a continuous bending, lifting, stretching, kneeling, and rising from one side of the lugger to the other. The dredges look like oversized garden rakes, each with a chain-and-nylon net attached, and are suspended by an iron frame. When one of these contraptions breaks the surface, looking vaguely like some prehistoric monster, the captain washes its haul of oysters in the boat's bow wave. The ancient chain and pulley scream as though being tortured while the heavy thing comes aboard over metal rollers. Oysters fall upon the deck with a hollow thud until the net has been shaken empty and the monster heaved overboard to continue its scavenging. The captain takes a moment just then to steer his vessel and maintain its circular path—but no more than a moment—before he is down on his hands and knees with a culling hammer, helping the crew break apart the clusters. Oysters come out of the dredges cemented to each other or to the remains of their ancestors. Under the mud that still clings, they look more like flat stones than the covering of what may be the most sensual food known to man.

The crew stay on hands and knees as the tap-tap of their hammers cleaves apart the mass of shells. Occasionally, the rhythm is broken as a beautifully patterned crab—a victim of the dredge—is tossed into a bucket for the night's meal or when the men stop to shovel the growing pile of oysters into a wire basket. When the basket is full, they stretch a burlap bag over its top and heave the whole thing upward and over until the limp strands are near to bursting. Except for interruptions, the tap-tapping is so persistent that the momentary pause is felt as a stillness, regardless of the groaning winches, the rumbling engines, and the shouted banter.

For two days, from before dawn until nightfall, the luggers circled up and down Buckskin Bayou. When the Daisys turned the expedition back toward Bayou du Large, they had a cargo of several hundred sacks of oysters, worth a couple of thousand dollars. The small, precise rhythms of culling and the grander ones of circling will be repeated virtually every day of the year except on Sundays and during the trapping season.

Under perfect conditions, an acre of oyster reef should produce three thousand dollars of oysters per year. But the ideal is rarely the actual. For all their rocklike outer appearance, oysters are delicate creatures. If the water they live in suddenly receives too much silt, they die within a few days. Jim has had grim experience with the vulnerability of oysters. During the spring of 1973, when runoff from the north surged into Louisiana and then rampaged through the long straight oil canals that cut through the marsh, the water in Buckskin Bayou turned cloudy with suspended debris and Jim lost the produce from two hundred acres of reefs.

"I'll tell you—you can never be happy in this business. I guess it's like anything aroun' here. If you does well one year, you're gonna do bad the next. I didn't think that water was gonna come in so dirty like that. I went out to the reef to dredge an' I got plenty of oysters, but they was all opened up. I jus' shook my head an' I said to myself, 'Well, Jim, yer jus' gonna have to wait till next year before you can buy that new lugger.' But I'll tell you something. That never happened to me before an' I been doin' this a long time. I think it's them canals they put in; it does something to the water, the way it goes down into the Gulf, you know what I mean?"

The well-being of oysters in Louisiana has been of considerable concern to scientists and businessmen alike. Fragile animals oysters may be, but they are important in the economics of the local seafood industry. A temporary surge of silt-laden water across their beds is only one of their problems. Of far greater consequence is the encroachment of salt water owing to the sinking of the marsh. It is not that oysters are intolerant of salt; they taste better after filtering it through their gills for a spell. The problem is that saline water is the habitat of three harsh predators—the oyster drill, the black drumfish, and a fungus known to science as *Labyrinthomyxa marinum*. As more and more of the traditional oyster beds come under the saline influence of the Gulf, oysters increasingly fall prey to one or another. The fungus merely weakens an oyster, but it can contribute to death if the oyster's resistance is already low. The two other predators simply ravage the oyster beds. A school of drumfish does it quickly and with such thoroughness that nothing is left but pulverized shells. The oyster drill—a periwinkle no more than four inches long—works by stealth, moving slowly over a reef, drilling tiny holes, and sucking out the meat from the shell. Oystermen used to fence in their reefs to keep out the drum, but the big, thick-headed fish can easily butt its way through wire mesh or cane poles. Such fences are now illegal because they are thought to interfere with the oil industry's tugs and barges. Oystermen have been left with no protection. Drumfish, sensitive to turmoil in their environment, usually sniff out an oyster bed that has just been disturbed, either by the propeller of a tug scraping over a reef or by an oysterman who has transplanted his oysters to saline water to improve their taste before harvesting. When an oysterman discovers that a school of drum is scavenging the vicinity, he stands vigil over his reef. Once the water begins to roll and surge with drum tails, he begins dredging and does not stop until the entire reef is cleaned out. Who will win the race is always a toss-up.

The efforts to prevent loss from oyster drills are more subtle. Palmetto fronds are tethered to stakes around the periphery of a reef, in the hope that drills will take refuge and lay their eggs in the leaves' dark crevices. Every so often an oysterman will pick up the fronds and shake them out. The drills that tumble out by the hundreds onto the deck of his lugger are edible and will provide him with a meal or two.

But the sinking of the marsh has made such preventive measures largely futile. The increased number of saline estuaries gives the predators access to hundreds of reefs. Oystermen now seed beds far inland where the water is still relatively free of them. But here the problem is pollution from industry and residential sewage. Practically all of south Louisiana's effluents flow into the estuaries. By the time they reach the Gulf, bacteria counts are ordinarily low enough to pose no danger to human health. But within the boundaries of the estuaries, counts are much higher, especially near areas where the marsh has been forced to give way to shopping centers and subdivisions. The state has been forced to close thousands of acres of reefs as a consequence.

The trip from Buckskin Bayou is a long one—hour after hour of chugging back across Lake Mechant and up the meanders of Bayou du Large to the line of houses that makes up Jim's community. Lake Mechant lives up to its name, which means "cruel lake," as the head wind sends scudding rollers crashing against the luggers' flared bows and onto their decks. The boats tumble into the troughs and hit against the lake's muddy bottom. There is no sign of human beings save for the floats of crab traps sprinkled over the frothing surface. Given the slowness of the boats and the absence of human intervention, the trip is much the same as it would have been a century ago. Several hours after leaving Buckskin Bayou, the first signs of civilization come into view—lonely buildings on skinny legs above a spit of land on the edge of Lake Mechant, looking as fragile as sandpipers. On summer and fall weekends, fishermen and hunters crowd into the camps and roar around the lake and the bayous in their outboards. Jim shakes his head when he speaks of them. All the camps follow the same design—a cabin, usually painted green, with a slightly pitched roof and a cypress wood cistern off to one side; a dock jutting into the bayou; and a boardwalk joining the dock to the cabin. Many of the buildings have incongruously silly names painted above their doors—Kitty Kat Two, Home on the Bayou, Poochie's Retreat, Heart's Throb. Now they are all deserted, their docks empty of boats and life-preserver-garbed children, windows shuttered, doors padlocked. Their silence blends with the desolation of the marsh. It occurs to me that the little colony might be a colonial outpost, a failed experiment about to yield to the way of the marsh in disposing of unwanted objects.

As the luggers move from the lake into the calmly flowing waters of Bayou du Large, the colony vanishes around the bend far more quickly than it appeared. Only a sagging electricity line is visible as evidence of human penetration into this hostile region. Willow and hackberry trees grow along the levees, interspersed with palmettoes just above the cattle-shorn grass. The stubby palms with their richly green, fan-shaped leaves have a prehistoric look that is reinforced by the acres of coarse marsh grass stretching beyond the levees. We are passing through a forgotten world, nibbled at by floods and cattle, abandoned by humanity except for a thin electrical line that for the time being serves no purpose.

But civilization is sure to come. Along the bayou, the first house is apparently of pioneer vintage—a tiny structure covered with light brown asphalt shingles, roofed with tin strips, its cockeyed door painted aquamarine. The ground in front, which slopes toward a wharf, has been rooted up by pigs and clucked over by nesting hens. Now, only a lone mongrel is to be seen. The wharf's pilings are twisted and gnarled and its planks treacherously pitted with holes. Barnacle-encrusted whitewall tires buffer it at the edge. Back of the house, cattle with some zebu in their lineage and horses with exposed ribs rub against a fence patchworked together out of tires, planks, logs, milk crates, and netting, as though everything floating down the bayou had been snagged for that makeshift purpose.

At the end of the Bayou du Large road half a mile farther up the bayou, a tumbledown tin boat shed leans above the water on rotted pilings. Fifty yards beyond, the half-submerged and much rotted hull of the *McMarie,* probably a fine oyster lugger in her day, lies careened on the mud, no more graceful now than the two rusting refrigerators and the one ancient stove that are her neighbors.

Trucks hauling oysters lurch along the pavement of what now looks like any other two-lane road. The docks are filled with people waving the luggers homeward.

"How did you do there, Jim? You look like you got a few sacks on them boats all right."

"Them oysters taste good an' salty? They got a truck up there near yer house."

"Yer first time out an' you done cleaned out yer reefs. You can take the rest of the year off."

Oyster luggers by the dozen line the bayou below the road, and

piles of oyster shells are a midden for future archeologists. Finally,
the towering shrimp boats, *Miss Lisa, Mr. Reese,* and *Little Kelly,*
come into view, so grand in appearance that they seem to overpower
the bayou itself. Little houses like Jim's line the road, tucked close
together. A school bus stops every few hundred yards to let off children who, though they look like any other American children, will
grow up to be trappers, shrimp- and oystermen, and boat builders
like their fathers and older brothers.

The three Daisy luggers come to a halt, edging into their particular notch in the bank, where the long string of craft is as much a part of the scene as the willows that shade the levees. The wives and children of the crew are waiting. Other relatives stroll up and stare at the sacks. Rachel comes across the street, a smile on her young face. Willie Junior races up to his father, who swings him high in the air, and then goes rushing from relative to relative for more of the same. Neighbors flock around in welcoming and curiosity over how Jim Daisy's oyster season has begun—milling about, staring at the sacks, asking Jim how his oysters are doing.

Ten minutes after the docking, a shiny-sided trailer truck from farther north backs up to a conveyor belt that leads to the luggers. The onlookers continue to mill about, eyes on the sacks that go up the belt and into the truck. Soon the big doors bang shut and the truck surges away to a stainless-steel complex where the oysters will be steamed open, washed, and canned. That world is far away from Bayou du Large, where technology is a temperamental accommodation between man and machine—man coaxing it along, machine responding with a groan. I wonder whether Jim feels the distance between that shiny truck and his own creaking luggers and dredges.

But as he turns away he says only, "We gotta get out there early tomorrow. I hope that weather don' turn cold. If that fog comes in, we ain't gonna be able to leave so early."

Nine

The Importance of Crawfish

Each spring, thoughts of crawfish fill the heads of most people in south Louisiana. As the leaves burst out and the warm breezes fan the countryside, speculation grows about how these small crustaceans have fared during the winter. Groups of bayou dwellers huddle about the water's edge in ever more earnest conversation about the extent of the spring runoff, the prices of previous seasons, and the quality of the meat. Mostly they talk about the price, still ridiculously low compared with that of other shellfish. Fifty cents a pound for live crawfish is about average, although it can go up to $1.25 a pound or drop to thirty-five cents. The price is usually highest in early spring, when only a small number have emerged from their mud burrows.

During these weeks before the runoff, old-timers groan as they recall their youth, when the price was five cents a pound, and say the industry is doomed. Fish-market owners meanwhile wring their hands, consumers curse their addiction to crawfish, and the crawfishermen gloat. As the water slowly rises and the price drops, people forget their complaints, buy a couple of sacks, and invite friends and relatives over for a night of happy gorging.

One of the most important differences between southern and northern Louisianans is that the latter do not eat crawfish. Many of them turn up their noses at the mention of it. In south Louisiana, on the other hand, passion for the creature verges on the absurd—and so, it might seem, does the amount of work required to extract one small morsel of meat from the crawfish's shell-covered tail. The passion stems not from the taste alone, but also from the community festival the eating of crawfish seems to require. A traditional crawfish boil is far more than a meal; it is a social occasion that brings people together to consume quantities of boiled onions and potatoes, pitchers of beer, and reams of paper towels, leaving behind buckets of crawfish debris. The armor worn by crawfish necessitates a slow meal; even the nimblest fingers become frustrated. Nothing could suit the south Louisiana life style better.

Combativeness is another reason for the popularity of the crawfish. Only four inches long, it is a feisty little animal, raising its pincers at the slightest provocation. But in the end it is always the loser, a victim of the human palate. Once, feeling a surge of the respect a conqueror can experience, along with wonder at the persistence of those claws, I rescued half a dozen crawfish from a sackful that were about to be boiled, housed them in a plastic basin, and fed them on carrot sticks. Despite all this care, every time I approached, up would go their pincers, ready to crush the hand that fed them.

In a backhanded gesture, this diminutive and very distant cousin of the lobster has become the mascot of south Louisiana. It has been immortalized in the form of pins, bumper stickers, and shoulder patches bearing the ironic slogan, Vive l'Ecrivisse. Cajuns have taken the animal's courage as a symbol for their own cultural revival. Some years ago, the Cajun town of Breaux Bridge, on the edge of the Atchafalaya Swamp, declared itself the crawfish capital of the world. Every two years since then, a weekend has been devoted to a hugely successful festival, with mountains of crawfish devoured. The name south Louisianans call them by is peculiar to the region. Just about everywhere else, they are known as crayfish.

Outsiders may have heard rumors of the mania for crawfish in south Louisiana, but they can hardly grasp its essence and are certainly dumbfounded, as I was, by typical native advice, complete with Cajun accent, on how to eat them: "You squeezes de tail an' sucks de haid." Louisiana is said to produce 99 percent of this country's crawfish harvest, an amount that may be anything from six to twenty million pounds depending upon climatic conditions. About 88 percent of the total stays right in south Louisiana. Part of the rest is shipped to Atlanta, Georgia, where crawfish eating has taken hold. Texans consume what the Georgians don't.

The United States is one of the few countries in the world that has never shown any widespread interest in crayfish as a source of food, even though a hundred species thrive in the lakes, rivers, and streams of North America. In parts of New Guinea, it is a staple. Europeans treat crayfish as a delicacy, all the more so since a fungus killed off most of the populations. In Austria, the animals were sometimes forced to walk through a mixture of cream and schnapps before being put to death so as to impart a richer flavor. In Finland, the eating of crayfish entails a strict code to be followed in dissection, using specialized instruments to extract the last shred of meat.

The fungus that destroyed the edible European species, *Astacus astacus,* except in isolated parts of Scandinavia, is endemic among the various North American species, thus providing them with immunity. How the fungus arrived in Europe is not known. At any rate, it first appeared in Italy during the 1860s. From there it swept through Europe and much of Asia, until strict limitations on the harvest were imposed, driving the price to such heights that for most people crayfish became a luxury of the past. Relief came from across the Atlantic, in the guise of *Pacifastacus leniusculus,* a species indigenous to the streams and lakes of California. It is larger than the species eaten in Louisiana, but of the same size and general proportions as the dwindling European stock. Swedish and Finnish researchers, recognizing a good thing, took it upon themselves to spirit away a few individuals from a Lake Tahoe research station to form the nucleus of what became a largely successful breeding program. They didn't share their knowledge with their European colleagues until a few years later. But then a former Austrian diplomat confessed that during his days of government service he had lowered his diplomatic pouch into the waters of Lake Tahoe and likewise smuggled out a few fertile crayfish, which he presented to biologists in Austria.

Whereas the European tradition of eating crayfish has a refined and painstaking etiquette, in Louisiana the tradition consists of eating as many of them as fast as possible, paying attention only to the tail meat and the juices in the head. Usually Louisiana crawfish are boiled in water heavily seasoned with cayenne, garlic, onions, and lemon. Tradition and the spicy dish itself demand quantities of beer to cool the palate. Indeed, beer drinking at a crawfish boil is as much a part of the cult as the crawfish themselves. The ultimate in the ethic of Louisiana crawfish eating is an eating contest. A contestant will easily do away with twenty-five pounds of crawfish, which comes to ten or so pounds of tail meat. Natives eating under normal conditions can gobble down five or six pounds of crawfish meat at a sitting. Crudity is part of the experience. At Red Richard's, a restaurant in the lovely town of Abbeville that serves nothing but crawfish, patrons sit at newspaper-covered tables, where they are brought great rectangular wash bins made of stainless steel, brimming with the bright red of boiled crawfish and decorated with onions and potatoes. Every so often, a waitress comes by with a garbage can and rips away the top layers of newspaper to clear a space for further accumulations of shell.

Like catfish, crawfish in this country have always been a poor man's food. One of the reasons the wealthy don't favor these two tender meats is misconstrued pride. All the aggrieved talk about the price of crawfish probably dates to their traditional consumers—people for whom a few pennies here and there really did make a difference. Before McDonald's came to Louisiana, crawfish were a spring and summertime staple for many families. Even today, some families rely on the crawfish they find in roadside ditches to provide a few free meals. On a spring weekend, battered cars line the soft shoulders of south Louisiana roads wherever a highway runs past a swamp. Their owners hover near the water, waiting for crawfish to fill the nets, while children and dogs run back and forth and the inevitable cans of beer are passed around.

The little nets used to dip for crawfish are probably unique to south Louisiana. Their quiet appearance in hardware and sporting-goods stores each spring is a symbol of that season no less than the blossoming of the camellias. The nets are merely squares of cotton mesh strung between the ends of two inverted-V-shaped wires somewhat thicker than the wire of a coat hanger. At the apex the wires join to make a neat handle that at once supports the net and holds it taut.

Crawfish are surprisingly fussy about bait. They like chicken necks, but prefer gizzard shad. Other kinds of meat they will only nibble on lethargically. A piece of shad in the middle of a net that is lowered into a drainage ditch is sure to be mobbed by as many crawfish as are in the vicinity. A dozen dip nets judiciously placed along a ditch, even one whose tired water is stained with oil at the surface, may produce a hundred pounds of crawfish a day.

Boiled crawfish is so thoroughly indigenous to the region that other methods of preparation tend to be restricted to special occasions. But they do exist. One of them is crawfish etouffée. I learned the recipe from Velma Ruiz, a Cajun woman with wide eyes and tightly pulled-back hair who is atypically proud of her heritage. She has much experience in the preparation of crawfish, since her husband, Woodrow, fishes for them part-time and is forever presenting her with a sackful.

She stood in her kitchen before a big bowl of pink, curled-up crawfish tails. Nearby was a smaller bowl full of a greenish, semiliquid stuff. "That's the key to good etouffée, right there in that bowl. That's the fat and that's what makes your roux take on a special taste." The fat, as she calls it, is actually the animal's liver and pancreas.

Like those of many Cajun women, her eyes beamed while her tongue wagged on the subject of cooking. "Now, you go to the best restaurant about here and you won't find etouffée that's worth half the money they charge for it. That's 'cause they don't use the fat. It's all in the fat. Some people don't like the taste of the fat. They say it's too oily, but those people aren't real crawfish lovers. If you don't like the fat, you don't really like crawfish."

The preparation of crawfish etouffée demands close attention—one reason so few people know how good it is. Another reason is that in order to create a proper etouffée one must commit a peculiar sort of murder. If "fat" in sufficient quantities is to be obtained, it must be extracted from the living animal. The process consists of removing the tail with a twist of the hands, ripping open the thorax—all the while trying to avoid the thrashing pincers, which can easily draw blood—and scooping out the greenish globules. The amount of guilt entailed depends on the amount of pain one believes the crawfish can experience. I prefer to think of it as quite limited. But who is to say? Yes, I am bothered by the idea of killing crawfish in so dreadful a manner, but then, by what right do I endow the crawfish with the pain I would experience at having my liver and pancreas ripped out. All I know is that the end result is delectable.

Most good Cajun cooking, etouffée included, depends upon the success of a roux, which consists of oil and flour cooked to a nutty brown richness. Into this goes the fat, together with scallions, chopped green pepper, parsley, and finally, the tails. "You just let it

bubble away there for a while and give it a sniff every so often until it smells and looks just right," Velma explained, following the impressionistic method that has given Cajun cooks their widespread reputation. "You'll know when it's ready; you'll just know, that's all."

Most of Louisiana's crawfish live in the Atchafalaya Swamp, which covers about half a million acres in the Atchafalaya Basin, the long shallow trough that runs down the center of south Louisiana. Fifty years ago the swamp and the basin were one and the same—two million acres of towering cypress and tupelo, hardwood stands, meandering channels, quiet pools, and sequestered lakes. But successive projects of levee building and channelization by the Army Corps of Engineers have turned swampland into farmland and reduced the swamp to a narrow finger along either shore of the Atchafalaya River. Even so, the swamp remains the most extensive such region in this country, no matter how troubled its future is by both past and prospective feats of engineering. The Army Corps of Engineers, backed by big landowners more interested in soybeans and cotton than in crawfish, has plans to dredge the river to ensure that potential agricultural land will never flood over. If this happens, the river may become nothing more than a huge sump for the tranquil backwaters of the swamp. Then not only will the crawfish disappear, but the swamp itself will give way to an onslaught of bulldozers and chain saws.

The swamp may die, even if the river is not dredged, a dilemma environmentalists find embarrassing. So much silt is flowing into the swamp from the Mississippi as a result of human manipulation that the swamp is becoming clogged. As the sediment collects on sandbars, filters among the willows, and fills in bayous, lakes have been transformed into miniature deserts. Where Grand Lake used to bend from the northern to the southern horizon, great sand flats have now emerged. Among forests of sprouting willows are glistening trunks of cypresses that were killed as the lake filled in.

Eighteenth-century pioneers who crossed the swamp from New Orleans to the fertile prairies of western Louisiana described the Atchafalaya as a dank place where the sunlight barely filtered through trees draped with Spanish moss. Alligators of enormous size were said to lurk on every bank, grinding their murderous ranks of teeth. Snapping turtles with shells the size of washtubs, and snakes the length of a pirogue, sunned themselves on logs amid the jagged knees of cypresses.

Even today, it becomes easy to imagine great sinister things waiting behind every tree or lying motionless on every rotting log. The stillness and clarity of the swamp, reflecting the trees above it in the light of early morning or late afternoon without the least blurring or distortion, are magical. Rot-resistant stumps of cypress trees felled years ago break the surface of the water with all their detail remaining, as though to bear witness against the overcutting the trees suffered. Each motion, each sound—the leap of a bass, the croak of an egret, even the rumble of a distant oil drill, comes as a vivid breach in the enormous tranquillity.

Shapes are so well defined here that camouflage seems a futile extravagance of nature. The tight coils of a cottonmouth are quite distinct from the contours of the log upon which it soaks up the sun. A great blue heron's long neck and legs, against the greenery, cancel the concealing possibility of the bird's coloration. Even the crawfish do not hide themselves. When the oxygen content of the water is low, they cluster around every stump and log in broad daylight, disappearing with flicks of their tails at the least disturbance.

The silence of the swamp discourages conversation, as though any spoken word were a blot on the purity. The denser the vegetation, the more overwhelming the stillness. Along barely discernible trails hewn out long ago by cypress loggers, the quiet suggests the moment before a thunderstorm breaks—intense, steaming, ready to burst with expectation. It takes time to realize that nothing is about to explode, that the mood of the swamp is one of perpetual waiting.

Woodrow Ruiz knows the passages through the swamp like he knows the lines in his hand. He was born and grew up there. As we drove along the levee that separates the world of sugarcane fields and ranch houses from the fantasy of the swamp's sprawling vegetation, I asked him if he ever got lost in it. Lifting his heavy Spanish eyebrows and laughing, he said in his thick Cajun accent, "Me, why no. I only get lost in cities. Here, I growed up right in the middle of the cypress. The whole swamp was my playground. Now, I go into Lafayette an' turn the corner an' it looks all strange and funny. I thinks to myself that I'll never find my way out."

Woodrow's father, Russell, used to cut cypress in the Atchafalaya and lived in a houseboat at the heart of the swamp for months at a time. Such men were called "swampers." The cycle of the seasons, the tremendous numbers of birds, and the crawfish were Woodrow's education. "I learned everything from this here swamp, me. I never did get no schoolin'. When I was a kid, me an' my friends would spend days jus' pokin' around the swamp, comin' back to the houseboat to sleep. I jus' 'bout scared my daddy to death sometimes when I was goned for a long time. But I learned a lot out there."

Now, some thirty years later, Woodrow is still drawn to the swamp's mysteries. He no longer lives there, but in a fine brick home in Loreauville, a little town on the banks of the Teche. It has a two-car garage, and the lawn is green and closely cropped. Inside, the furniture is luxurious, the kitchen modern; thick carpeting stretches from one wall to another. It was the oil industry that made possible such comfort for Woodrow. For years he has worked as a roustabout. Starting off on a seven-and-seven schedule, he was later promoted to a job that runs from nine to five, five days a week. "Those oil people been good to me. I worked for it, but they treated me nice. Still, I like the swamp. I get in it every time I can. You ask my wife." Woodrow let out a long chuckle as the truck bounced along the rough road to Ruiz Landing, where he was going to put his boat in the water. For years after his father left the swamp, he ran a little general store at the landing. Then the Army Corps of Engineers made him move off the levee because they wanted to pile more swamp muck on top of it for reinforcement. "Yessir, every time I get the chance, I head for the swamp. They give me a two-week vacation every year, an' I spend it here, out every day. An' in the spring during the crawfish season, I set my traps every Friday night an' run 'em Saturday and Sunday. I been doin' that for years. If I knewed that there would be a lot of crawfish every year, I'd quit my job an' just fish for crawfish. Of course, the swamp's changin' now with all this silt an' stuff comin' in. I don't know what it's gonna be like in ten years."

Just as the marsh gets into the blood of trappers, the swamp binds crawfishermen to it. Most families living around the edges of the swamp have at least one member who feels as Woodrow does. That adds up to a considerable number of people. Lines of pickup trucks could be seen parked all along the levee that guards the swamp's seclusion. Most of these belonged to crawfishermen who were already running lines of traps in some private corner of the swamp they had discovered.

In Woodrow's outboard, we roared down one canal and then another, swerving back and forth to avoid deadheads and branches. Snakes the diameter of a man's wrist slithered off logs, and a barred owl veered through the cypress as softly as a moth over a fresh-cut lawn. Suddenly we shot out of the narrow channels and were in the Atchafalaya River itself, wide and muddy, full of swirling eddies and tree stumps carried all the way from Idaho or Wisconsin or western New York State or any of a number of places. The hidden currents in the river are vicious for any helmsman, and many a boat has capsized and gone to the bottom within minutes. In some spots, the river is two hundred feet deep. Woodrow didn't seem to pay much heed to its reputation. He just gunned the outboard across the current.

He pointed the bow toward a stand of young willows that fringed the opposite side with their supple foliage and pushed the engine still further open. With a smile of Cajun delight, he yelled, "Watch yerself now. We're gonna part them willows down the middle." Young willows though these were, their trunks, growing out of the water, looked sturdy enough to snag a light aluminum hull. We hit the trees at forty miles an hour and all I could see was greenery bending away from the boat's prow as though nature were bowing to our passage. Suddenly the stand of young willows gave way to a domain of other, statelier trees, their trunks arching up out of the murky water like figures in a sculpture garden. Here among them was Woodrow's crawfish-hunting ground, the location of each of his sixty traps marked by a blue plastic ribbon attached to a branch, from which a line descended into the water.

The season had been one of the best in recent memory. The evidence was there as Woodrow pulled his traps up. Most were full of struggling red swamp crawfish, the predominant species in Louisiana, along with the skeletons of gizzard shad whose meat had been devoured the night before. Some of the traps also held water snakes, their drowned and contorted bodies intricately snared in the chicken wire to which they had been attracted by the presence of what must have looked like such a feast.

Woodrow was a happy man that morning, smiling and chuckling from the stern of his boat in the middle of the swamp. He approached each trap with the fervor of the hunt, relieving the tension with such declarations as, "We're gonna be overflowin' with crawfish after we pull up this here, I do believe," or "Yesterday, this one here was brimming full and I bet you it's going to be the same today." He treated his prisoners like kin. When one clung to the side of a trap after the rest had been shaken into a bucket, Woodrow would implore, "Com'on out of there, cher, come on into the boat and join yer friends." And if a crawfish fell from the bucket into the boat's bilge, he would say as he grasped it, "Now where do you think you goin'? You think you can put a hole right through my boat an' escape? No sir, it ain't easy like that."

By midmorning, six onion sacks were full of crawfish hissing and crackling, thousands of them altogether. Each sack weighed about forty pounds, and at that time each pound was worth forty cents. If Woodrow had sold them all, he would have grossed almost four hundred dollars for a morning's work. But he sold only a few, giving the rest away to relatives, friends, and neighbors in perpetuation of the old reciprocity.

Only minor fluctuations in the climate will turn a potentially rich harvest into a poor one such as can set bayou conversation humming for weeks. As it is, the swamp produces a good crawfish harvest on an average of only two years out of five. During one of the rare good seasons, a crawfisherman may make forty or fifty thousand dollars for three or four months of work. But those extravagant earnings be-

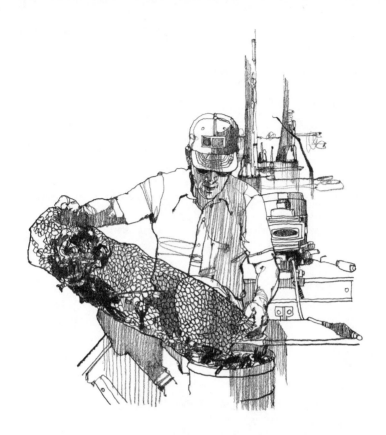

come a reminder that other years are not so lucrative. For years before, the water had been low and crawfish were scarce. Those who traditionally pursued them were obliged to pull their traps early and take to other occupations—hoop-net fishing, running a trotline, or, if they were sufficiently desperate, frogging or turtling.

Any crawfisherman knows that the three climatic prerequisites for a bumper harvest are a dry summer, a wet fall, and a mild winter. Louisiana's two commercial species—the red swamp and the white river crawfish—spend a good part of the year underground. In late spring or early summer, as the runoff flows away to the Gulf and the interior of the swamp turns into a mud-floored willow forest, crawfish by the billions burrow little tunnels in the rich, heavy muck, driven by an instinct that causes them to seek moisture. They sometimes dig down more than three feet, a remarkable achievement for pincers and spindly legs that are seemingly unequipped for digging. More remarkably still, crawfish are builders as well as excavators. Before taking up residence underground, they wall each burrow to a height of three or four inches with mud brought up from the hole into what south Louisianans call a chimney. New crawfish settlements are discernible by the clusters of chimneys that spring up overnight across a mud flat or, not infrequently, across the lawn of a low-lying house.

While the digging is in progress, crawfish mate, in a not very affectionate manner. After the male has deposited the sperm in an external sac on the underside of the female's tail, she vanishes into her den, sometimes followed by her mate, and pulls an ill-fitting door of mud over the chimney opening. There, either the two of them, or the female alone, remain for three or four months before she lays her eggs, between three hundred and seven hundred of them, each fertilized by the contents of the sperm sac.

As fast as the female produces the eggs, they become glued to the bottom of her tail, forming a sticky cluster. By now it is early fall. The eggs hatch after two or three weeks and quickly begin developing into creatures half an inch long but no thicker than a pencil lead. Their survival now depends upon a rise in the water level that will permit them to escape from the burrow and begin their own lives. The vegetation that a dry summer has permitted to spring up on mud flats is their first food.

If water levels do not rise very greatly during the fall, the parents will remain near their burrow. The coming of winter drives them into the seclusion of the den, and during the cold winter months the close quarters produce either stress or hunger. Researchers who have broken into the burrows have discovered only females. The rumored cannibalistic tendencies of crawfish would seem to be confirmed by the mysterious disappearance of the males.

If the winter is too harsh, the survival of the young crawfish becomes doubtful if not impossible. When the temperature drops below fifty-five degrees Fahrenheit for long periods, young crawfish go into a state of semi-hibernation that makes them easy targets for birds and fish, as well as inhibiting their growth, and in the ensuing spring, the dearth of crawfish will again be a source of complaint in south Louisiana.

The same complaints will be heard if the spring runoff is slight or doesn't occur at all. Still in their winter burrows, adult crawfish—or those that have not been eaten by their mates—may peep out, but if the melting snows from the north have not filled their swampland bathtub to the brim, they will simply retreat and wait out the dry period. Low water will completely upset the annual schedule of the young crawfish. If the water doesn't rise in the spring, they begin the arduous task of digging out burrows as much as four months earlier than normal. There, like their parents, they will hide and wait for the high water. And south Louisianans will throw up their hands in despair.

There are now commercial crawfish farms, begun in an effort to counteract the whims of nature. By the late 1970s they accounted for 40 percent of the annual harvest. Rice farmers have long thought of the barbed crustaceans as possessing mysterious powers because of their way of suddenly appearing in fields even though the surrounding land may be high and dry. But it is after the summer harvest, when combines have turned fields into a terrain of miniature mountain ridges and deep ravines, that the crawfish unintentionally reveal themselves as the farmer's helpmates. During the harvest, they have been snuggled away in their burrow villages; but once the combines have gone, they emerge to fill in the valleys and smooth out the mountains with their ceaseless nocturnal comings and goings.

It was not until about two decades ago that rice farmers, turning the mystical appearance of the crawfish to their own financial benefit, began to sell them. A neat cycle of rice-crawfish-rice evolved. In April or May, when the young rice shoots are just beginning to turn the northern rim of the marsh a hazy green, farmers stock their flooded fields with crawfish. There the crustaceans find life easy. Tender shoots are plentiful; predators are few; the water level is constant. The crawfish can spend the whole summer there—foraging, growing, and finally mating. Before the rice harvest, fields are drained. As water levels drop, crawfish begin burrowing, following the instinct of eons. In the seclusion of their dens, they also avoid the mechanical traumas overhead as the rice is cut. Later, in the tranquillity of autumn, fields are reflooded, solely for the benefit of the crawfish. Undisturbed, they lay their eggs and hatch out their young, which are assured a comfortable winter of steady water levels, with rice stubble to feed on. By late winter the fast-growing younger generation is tender and ripe for the boiling pot.

For environmental purists, the tandem growing of rice and craw-fish has a further advantage. Crawfish, invertebrates distantly related to beetles, spiders, and a host of other insects, are extremely vulnerable to the pesticides and chemical fertilizers upon which food growers in a technological society are so dependent. Farmers who spray their new shoots with some pesticides soon find their fields empty of crawfish. In the interest of their second crop, rice-crawfish farmers are thus forced to join the ranks of organic food producers. Over the past years, however, crawfish farming has begun to remove itself from dependence on the rice-growing cycle and to occupy a place of its own. There are now thousands of acres of man-made ponds in south Louisiana devoted exclusively to raising crawfish. Water levels are adjusted to encourage growth and fecundity, food and minerals are poured into the water, and the crawfish are trapped according to a schedule conceived with an eye to the market. Crawfish that have been so thoroughly pampered taste different from their wild brethren, of course. Woodrow is scornful. "They got nothin' to 'em," he says. "They're like pap. Their meat is soft an' mushy. An' they don' have the taste like the wild ones. Give me a wild crawfish any day."

The Louisiana crawfish industry is just beginning. Researchers are stepping up their efforts to make farm-raised crawfish the rule rather

than the exception. Processing engineers are talking about designing machines that will extract the pink tail meat from the thrashing animal in minutes. The days of the demand for wild crawfish are numbered—as are the days when crawfish eating was restricted almost entirely to Louisiana. Frozen crawfish may soon be as common as frozen shrimp. It will be too bad for those people in the North, or anywhere outside south Louisiana for that matter, to sit down to a meal of fried crawfish tails without knowing anything of the swamp creature whose combativeness is so much a part of the lore of south Louisiana.

Ten

Shrimp Fever

In south Louisiana, the transition from winter to summer lasts only a few weeks. During those weeks the marsh has turned green, birds have begun raising their young, alligators are cruising the bayous, and levees have started to dry up. The pace of life becomes frenzied. Farmers work from before sunrise until far into the night. There are rice paddies to be planted, sugarcane fields to be plowed, land for soybeans to be cleared, and equipment to be repaired. When all this is done, the only thing left to do is wait for the shrimping.

The spring season for shrimps opens each year toward the end of May, but preparations are likely to have begun months before. The first sign is the laying out of timbers in front yards, following boat plans scrawled on napkins after a winter's meal. Eventually the wood, which is almost always cypress, has been cut to a keelson and ribs, which are customarily laid on four oil drums of varying colors. These supports are crucial to the construction of a shrimp boat. They will be a cradle for the growing boat until it is launched. For months, the work proceeds casually—a plank here, a plank there. Around the end of March, the pace quickens; with the help of neighbors and relatives, a boat begins to take shape, evolving day by day from a mere framework of naked sticks to a full-fleshed hull. It is invariably well constructed, since the people of the bayous grow up knowing about boat building and the stresses a vessel must endure. One day during the first weeks of April, neighbors gather to roll the new hull into the bayou. These gatherings are a common sight at this time of year.

Most of the boats are Lafitte skiffs, a graceful design whose lines are adapted to the local ecology. It was first used in the early years of the century by shrimp fishermen from the small bayou settlement of Lafitte, whose work in the open-water shallows of Barataria Bay required a craft that could withstand swells driven by a south wind. One hallmark of the skiff is beaminess. A twenty-foot-long hull with an eight-foot beam suggests an ungainly appearance; but its curves are beguiling to the eye. The bow widens aft as softly as a child's cheeks; the gunwales amidships slope toward the waterline with a gentle pitch; and the wide stern overhangs the rest of the boat with a casual elegance.

Lafitte skiffs are not the only boats used by shrimpers. Larger vessels of a very different sort go far out into the Gulf. These tower at the bow and have flared gunwales, a low transom to facilitate bringing aboard the catch, and a wide square stern. The design was brought to Louisiana from Florida, where deep-water trawling long dominated the industry. Louisiana shrimpers did not venture far offshore until after 1938, when tremendous shoals of white shrimps were discovered in the deep water off Morgan City. The Lafitte skiff and the Florida trawler are the two classic shrimping craft, but Louisianans by no means restrict themselves to classic forms. The opening of the season brings out any number of nautical concoctions, which constitute a motley parade down the bayous to the shrimping grounds. The only pieces of standardized equipment are the trawls and the door boards, two squares of weighted wood that force the jaws of the trawl open as it scrapes across the bottom.

During the weeks just before the "opening," as it is called, there are signs of tension among bayou dwellers. The pace of preparation—boats taking shape, door boards being painstakingly crafted and balanced, nets being repaired—may go haywire as the question of when the Wildlife and Fisheries Commission will declare the season open remains unanswered. Shrimping in Louisiana is big business. In 1977, an exceptionally good year, almost seventy million pounds were processed, and were worth almost a hundred million dollars to shrimp fishermen. To these people, the opening is like a stampede to the gold fields.

Along with being the highest shrimp-producing area in the country (an honor shared with Texas), Louisiana's millions of acres of estuaries are also the most lavish nursery in the United States. To set the opening date of the spring season requires some sensitivity toward both the growth rate of the young shrimps and the impatience of fishermen and the business community dependent on shrimping. Invariably, commercial interests hound the commissioners to open the season early, and the commissioners, advised by biologists, offer statistics that suggest it should be opened later. The usual outcome is a compromise. Yet some rules are observed. The principal one governs the weight of the young brown shrimps that have spent the early spring growing in the estuaries—one hundred of their number must weigh at least a pound. It is not so unusual, however, for a fisherman to set his trawl on the sly, some moonless night before the opening date; the local bayou people gladly buy his catch without a whisper of reproach.

The two most important commercial shrimp species in the state are the brown and the white shrimps, known collectively as penaeids (from the Latin word *penna*) in reference to their feathery grace. Pink shrimps, royal reds, and sea bobs (a bastardization of the French words *six barbes*) are also penaeids, but are not of great commercial value in Louisiana. Brown and white shrimps, although similar in appearance, have some unmistakable differences, the principal one being in the timing of their reproductive cycles. This means that inshore shrimpers can trawl from late spring through late fall, with only a short midsummer break when the season is closed. More than three miles offshore, there are no restrictions on shrimping. All year round the big Florida trawlers wallow in the swells, looking lazy under the sun as they drag their hundred-foot trawls.

Both white and brown shrimps spawn throughout the year, but there are definite peaks in their reproductive cycles. Off the Louisiana coast, the brown shrimps mainly spawn during the early winter, and the white shrimps during the summer. The adult female of each species lays from half a million to one million eggs, which hatch almost immediately into the first of eleven planktonic stages through which young shrimps go before reaching larval shape and begin to look like shrimps. While these changes are taking place, something else is happening that is even more remarkable—a migration so dumbfounding that it borders on the mystical, continuing to baffle scientists who have studied it for years. The larvae, as they roll about in the waters of the Gulf, find their way from the open sea, through the narrow passes between the barrier islands, across the shallow and

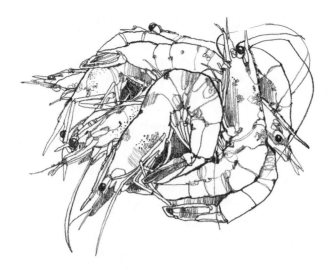

choppy waters of the bays, and into the nourishing embrace of the estuaries. The journey sometimes covers fifty miles and takes from three to five weeks. Billions of larvae die during this time. Currents and tides undoubtedly have a part in the migration, but scientific opinion has been obliged to give the larvae credit for finding their own way landward.

Brown shrimp larvae arrive in the estuaries in waves beginning in January and continuing through April. They spend from two to four months in the protective shallow water at the edge of the marsh, feeding and growing on the zooplankton and bits and pieces of decaying vegetation, which are all plentiful. But when the shrimps are an inch or two long, they start off on another journey—back to their birthplace in the Gulf. Though the process is again not well understood, thousands of fishermen take advantage of it, descending on the shrimps as they pass through the bays into deeper water. The seaward migration is no reluctant dribble, but a mass movement. Shrimps surge out of the shallow water, often carried by the tide when the moon is full, and gather in countless numbers in the bays, known to biologists during such times as "staging areas." When the season has favored the survival and growth of the young shrimps, the bays are so filled with them that they boil to the surface. For weeks, they continue to stream out of the narrow passes and into the Gulf. At night during this period, fishermen sometimes gather by the hundreds in the passes, where they scoop out the shrimps by the tons with nets known locally as *paupières*. In French the word means "eyelids," and any fisherman will tell you that the nets really should be *papillons,* for "butterflies," since the outline of the upraised nets on the stern of a vessel does suggest wings of a gigantic but delicate butterfly. But local people shrug off the discrepancy, as if language could matter when the shrimps are running. The butterfly-shaped net consists of a fine mesh supported on a rectangular frame made of metal. One corner of the net is usually hinged to a boat's gunwale, or sometimes to the edge of a dock, and lowered into the water to a depth of three or four feet. Since shrimps swim near the surface at night, this is an easy way to fish—merely pulling the net up, emptying it, and then dropping it again. The ultimate experience for a shrimp fisherman is to be at a pass when the moon is full and the night is calm and clear. In a few hours under those circumstances, he can catch more shrimps than he could in weeks of trawling.

Shrimping in Louisiana began in the estuaries, first by seining (a back-breaking method), next by trawling from sailing luggers, and finally by trawling from motorized Lafitte skiffs. Up until thirty years ago, shrimping was always a small-time operation. But once the offshore schools of shrimps began to be exploited, the industry developed an elaborate technology. The big boats require complex machinery, communications equipment, and refrigeration; they are away from their home ports for weeks at a time. Inshore shrimping is grounded on informality and tradition; often the commercial fishermen are brothers or cousins of those who just want to fill their own freezers.

The shrimp season invariably opens at one minute after midnight. For the people who have camps on Boston Canal, that evening is the most exciting time of the whole year. From its wintertime isolation, with the members of the Stelly family as the sole residents, Boston Canal is now turned into an old-time bayou community. Messages in Cajun accents are carried across the roiled water:

"I got me a new trawl this year, me. She sure to work good, I guarantee."

"You hear that them wildlife people catched some shrimp thirty to the pound. Those must by purty shrimp."

"You wait till tonight an' you'll see some purty shrimp."

Whether or not the shrimp will be "purty" is the question that runs from boat to levee and back again as Boston Canal fills with shrimpers. The dock in front of the Stellys' cabin quivers with scurrying feet as the owners and crews of four or five boats—friends and relatives of Clifford Stelly—make last-minute checks, repair running lights, tie new bags onto trawls, break up ice in the chests, and fine-tune their engines. Children, even more than adults, become vehicles of the excitement that vibrates all along the canal. Their voices drift over the water long after dark, while the yellow gleam of the anti-mosquito lights on the docks invests their scampering bodies with a ghostly tint.

The wait until midnight is long, and the intervening hours are full of uncertainty. In the Stellys' cabin, men sit around the little kitchen table with ears cocked toward the CB radio. Stelly women pad about in scuffed slippers, emptying ashtrays and serving coffee. The generator, rhythmically pounding out in the back, causes the lights to flicker across faces in a visible pulse. From time to time, garbled voices on the CB report that the season will be a light one, that the shrimps are going to be small and scarce. Whenever a new statement crackles through the room, the men lean forward in their chairs, the sudden movement stirring up layers of cigarette smoke that hang about their heads. All the months of preparation are about to be tested, and the men are worried.

"Ah dunno what to think," says Clifford, leaning back in his chair and rubbing his hands back and forth along the tops of his thighs. "Two weeks ago, they tol' us there were gonna be some purty shrimp an' now look what they sayin'."

"I bet they got some purty ones out there," Della reassures from the sink. "Babineaux says he seen some good ones."

"Well, I'm ready for any of 'em what's out there," one of Clifford's friends declares. "I got that motor so it jus' purrs. She ain't gonna die on me like she done las' year, ah'll tell you."

"I wonder how my bag's gonna do. I jus' tied her to my trawl. She looks good," says another friend whose name is Percy. All skin and bones, he teeters at the edge of a chair like a starling on a wire. "Hey, Cliff, how do those door boards look? They look good?"

"Yeah, they look real good. You done 'em real nice. I think they got good balance," Clifford replies with a nod. Marsh neighbors for many years with only three or four miles of grass as a shared back-yard, Percy and Clifford are forever doing each other favors. A pair of shiny new door boards is Percy's latest gift.

Percy is just now the rather shamefaced hero of Boston Canal.

Two weeks ago, Wildlife and Fisheries Commission agents caught him trawling for shrimps in the dead of night. "It was right out in front of my camp." He recounts the story with pride, now that most of the residents of the canal have put aside their snickers and are resigned to hearing his version of the story. "That night was black, black. I wasn't usin' no lights a-tall. I'd made two or three passes an', boy, was those shrimp somethin' purty. I must a had me forty pounds. All of a sudden, this big light hits me right in the face. I thought the world had blowed up. But then I knew what was happenin'. The agents came up, they was two, an one of 'em says, 'Don' you know that the season ain't open?' An' I says,''Course, I know that; you think I'm stupid?' Well, they took away my trawl an' boards but they let me keep the shrimp. Were they ever purty. I thought that was all right of 'em. They jus' give me back the trawl yesterday."

The story still brings a few chuckles, but at its conclusion there is silence. Clifford turns the subject back to the present: "Ah sure hope them shrimp are as purty tonight as they was then."

After a while, conversations come to an end. Eyes turn disinterestedly toward the television, where Charlie's Angels are flirtatiously thwarting some maniac's scheme to murder a group of Arab oil sheiks while they watch the Icecapades. Randall Stelly goes out with a flashlight to "bull-eye" some alligators in the crevey back of the camp. I jump up, eager to accompany him as a distraction from the waiting. Unlike the glumly apprehensive occupants of the camp, the garfish in the crevey are turning cartwheels of excitement in the murky water where young shrimps are abundant. They roll to the surface, their torpedo-shaped bodies twisting, mouths agape, and with powerful thrusts of the tail.

The eyes of the marsh dwellers come alive under the flashlight's powerful beam. It reflects the emerald eyes of two alligators, pure jewels in their setting of bone and leather. Pinpricks of green belong to frogs' eyes, and those of nutrias are of a pink so faint that you think you're imagining it until you see a dark form stealing from the edge of the water into a clump of marsh grass.

At a few minutes before midnight, the banks of Boston Canal awaken to the roaring of motors, the shouts of fishermen, and arcs of moving lights. The long wait has come to an end. Shrimp boats by the hundred plow down the canal to Vermilion Bay, following the same route as the billions of shrimps on their way to the Gulf. Well-wishers on the docks, yellow under the mosquito lights, wave fare-well and tell their husbands and sons to come back with purty shrimps.

The CB radio in Clifford's boat nearly explodes with excitement as friends report to each other the size of the catch in test trawls. The talk is garbled. "See them lights over by that rig. That's where we're at. A fella over here tells me he got a full test trawl jus' a few minutes ago. We're puttin' down now, ten-four."

Another voice comes in. "Hey, Bayou Boy, this here's the Otter an' ah'm over here by Red Fish Point an' the shrimp are boilin' up to the surface, at least ah seen a few shrimps on the surface. Ah'll call you back when we pull in."

Out in the bay, the wind freshens. Clifford's little eighteen-foot inboard bounces and buries its nose in the swells. Clifford's lips are set, and he leans forward at the wheel to peer through the spray-washed windshield. "Ah don' like this wind," he says. "It take all the fun out of trawlin' bouncin' aroun', not being able to see where you're going. It ain't like trappin'. Ah always knows where ah'm at then." The CB radio continues to spurt out garbled messages, full of questioning now the shrimps are so scarce.

"Pelican, you hear me, Pelican."

"Yeah, got ya, Mud Hen."

"Well, I jus' wanna say that we pulled in our test an' we got us two white shrimp an' about ten little browns. We're gonna head back an' come out in the morning. The shrimp'll be down on the bottom if the sun comes out good. I don' know why we ain't gettin' anything. Ten-four."

The lights that filled the bay just after midnight have receded to-ward the protection of the bayous. Clifford fidgets at the wheel and then announces that he's "gonna make a little pass." The decision gives him a sudden agility, and he bounds to the boat's overhanging stern and filters the trawl through his big hands into the waves. He throws out the tickler, a chain that drags on the bottom ahead of the trawl and alarms resting or feeding shrimp so that they flick them-selves upward and into the net's mouth; then he unhooks the new door boards.

Half an hour later, the sorting box in the boat's stern holds an as-sortment of marine life: small croakers, catfish, crabs, sea trout, and about ten shrimps. Clifford is frigidly silent as he sorts out the shrimps and crabs. He tilts up one end of the box so the "trash" slides into the waves. "Ah think we call it a night now," he says with a solemn voice. "Ah never seen anything this bad. We're not payin' for our gas this way."

The docks along Boston Canal are still crowded, but the crowd is silent now. Some of the boats' crews cup their hands to indicate a small catch as they pass a dock. Others just shrug their shoulders and shout tersely that they have other business to attend to. Those on the docks nod their heads in sympathy. Even the children are quiet. They watch their fathers and brothers tie up their boats and don't know whether they should say anything about what happened to the shrimps.

The marsh still holds its mysteries. No one along the canal is sure what happened to the shrimps in the spring of 1978. Most people don't even speculate. But some do venture a guess or two. They say it may be oil pollution from leaking wells, or maybe it is because of all the canals that have been cut through the marsh, or the growing number of summer weekend dwellers, the creep of subdivisions, the sewage that floats down the bayous. Ironically, no one mentions the most plausible explanation—that there are just too many fishermen. Fifteen years ago there were only six thousand licensed shrimp boats in the state that harvested around seventy million pounds of shrimps, heads off. Now there are twenty-two thousand licensed boats catching the same amount. Such pressure is sure to exhaust the shrimp population.

But people aren't used to the idea of finding no shrimps. They prefer to think those shrimps are lurking in the bay, just waiting for someone with the expertise to find them. That someone is likely to be Joe Broussard. If anyone can catch shrimps, the people along Boston Canal will say, it is Joe Broussard. He depends on shrimps for a living and can sniff out a school halfway across Vermilion Bay. He does so with the help of his beautiful Lafitte skiff, the *Miss Tee,* which carries a fifty-foot trawl. There is a huge sorting box in the bow, there are big square ice chests, and there is an awning that shades almost the entire cockpit—a necessity under the intense summer sun. The *Miss Tee*'s four-hundred-horsepower engine can take Joe anywhere in Vermilion Bay in less than an hour, and from Boston Canal out into the Gulf in just a little longer.

Joe trawling for shrimps radiates the same enthusiasm as Clifford when he traps. Four or five years ago, after a year of college—unusual in itself—had filled him with curiosity about more than marsh life, Joe ended up in Virginia working for a moving-van company. The experience proved a tormenting one. It was not long before Joe realized that he needed the marsh. So he came back. "Man, is *it* good to be here," he exclaimed to me one day as he showed off his boat. "The marsh is one place I'm never gonna leave again, no sir. I felt like everythin' was upside down when I was up there."

Joe's return to the marsh has established him as a hero along Boston Canal and the other bayou communities—a very different status from the temporary notoriety of his uncle Percy after his run-in with the game wardens. Instead of an ordinary CB name, one referring in some way to marsh life, Joe is grandly known as "the Pope." He bubbles with enthusiasm for whatever he does—not only shrimping, but trapping in winter, with a few sidelines such as car-body-repair work and bricklaying. Each spring he prances down the bayous aboard the *Miss Tee,* his arms waving, a grin crinkling his eyes, his talk full of wisecracks.

The day after the opening, I trawled with Joe in Vermilion Bay. By seven o'clcok in the morning, people knew he was in the area. "Where you at, Pope?" the CB repeatedly crackled. "You done any good yet?" Joe answered each question with a joke and a plea that he had not even had time to drop his trawl. "Hey, Snake Eyes, where were you las' night. I had so many shrimp in my boat that it was about to sink with all them waves. I was callin' all over for you to take some of my shrimp but they told me you went to bed early."

Joe headed the *Miss Tee* out into the middle of the bay, cutting through a fleet of big shrimp boats that looked like dragonflies as we crossed their bows. We could see their arms stretched over the calm water, each one dragging a trawl with lines taut as a spider's thread in the delicate morning light. Hoping that one of them had found a school, Joe dropped the test trawl. The result was one shrimp and one crab. "Hell, man, these boys don' know what they're doing. They jus' going around in circles for the fun of it. I'm going to my secret place. Just me an' the shrimp know about it. At least that's the way it was last fall." Joe wadded some snuff into his mouth and revved the boat toward his secret place. It turned out to be a totally unlikely spot for shrimps—a part of the bay encircled by ugly oil platforms, derricks, and their attendant barges, with a sheen of oil on the water. The modest shape of the shrimp trawl against the towering geometry of the derricks reminded me once again of how the haphazard life of the bayous still goes on side by side with the no-nonsense efficiency of the petroleum rigs.

Here, the shrimps were scarce, too. Joe's response to the nearly empty test trawl was a squirt of snuff-stained spit over the side. But optimism, a necessity of the hunt, does not die easily. "Screw this puny test trawl," he snarled, giving it a disdainful kick. "Let's drop the big one an' go whole hog. We're gonna catch us some shrimp."

With the trawl over the side, the *Miss Tee* lost her carefree grace and became a groaning workhorse. Shrimping is a slow business. Each pass lasts several hours and there is not much to do on that quiet bay except to wish for the next "pickup" when one can begin sorting the shrimps from the trash fish. The sun burns mercilessly, and the horizon has the baked look it can take on when the weather is hottest. Even under the shade of the awning, the heat will dry your throat if you inhale with your mouth open. Conversation is minimal. The engine's grumblings drown out anything softer than a scream. Waiting is all there is left to do, waiting and imagining that huge mouth below as its bottom lip scruffs up the mud, imagining the shrimp crowding against the unseen mesh of the net.

Finally Joe winched in his trawl. With a dip net he scooped up its contents into the sorting box. I was amazed. There were crabs galore, including a dozen helpless soft-shelled ones. The hard-shelled ones scuttled to the corners of the box, the big males' long-armed pincers clacking. Baby croakers, sea trout, flounders, and redfish poured into the box by the hundreds, easy victims for the crabs, which grasped anything soft. There were dead, leathery banana fish shaped uncannily like banana peels. A small snapping turtle plodded stoically through the confusion. A stingray snapped its barbed tail; drumfish and sheepshead clicked their teeth; and hard-headed catfish thrashed about, their venomous barbs outstretched. There were also shrimps—only a few, the polychrome tails of the big white ones adding another tint to all the silver-gray-brown of the fish. Brown shrimps were more numerous, but every one was small—too small for most shrimpers to bother with.

The white shrimps were about five inches long, the "purty" shrimps that had been the object of so much anticipation. Even though brown shrimps were the designated target of the just-opened season, it was white ones that shrimpers prized. Like their brown cousins, these were still growing and on their way out toward the Gulf when the trawl intercepted them. Biologists call these white shrimps "ghosts," because they had stayed behind when most of their generation were heading for deep water the previous fall. White shrimp larvae surge into estuaries all during early summer, overlapping at the start with the seaward migration of juvenile brown shrimps. Thus places like Vermilion Bay become two-way thoroughfares for the comings and goings of shrimps. Some white shrimp larvae have grown only a little when the first chilly days of fall cause the temperature of the shallow water to drop—the signal that drives the young shrimps toward the protection offered by the less fickle temperatures of deep water. But since food is scarce in those depths, the immature shrimps will not grow there. To reach maturity, they need additional food that only the estuaries can provide. Instinct apparently tells them this, for after spending a short time in the Gulf, they turn around and head back to the estuaries. This second migration to shallow water is the one that coincides with the brown shrimp larvae's annual migration. The undernourished white shrimps thus temporarily adapt themselves to the life style of the brown shrimps, feeding beside them in the estuaries, migrating side by side back to the Gulf, and winding up along with them in Joe Broussard's trawl.

Four hundred pounds of fish, dead and dying, gasping and convulsed in weakening flurries, filled the sorting box—the mysteries of deep water revealed. The first to go overboard were the big drumfish. One by one, Joe roughly gaffed them and cast them into the water. The catfish went next, followed by the stingray; the barbs of both species are a danger no shrimper wants to contend with. Joe flicked the snapping turtle over the gunwale without blinking. He saw it only as a hindrance. He dumped the hard-shelled crabs into a big basket to be sold later. The soft-shell crabs were gently put on ice for the evening meal.

Only shrimps and little fish were left, some of the latter still gasping. These were mere fingerlings—the croakers, sea trout, and redfish that have given Louisiana its name as a seafood capital. Joe paid no attention to them. His fingers picked nimbly through the mass in search of shrimp. When he had removed them, the dead fish were washed overboard with a couple of buckets of water. Their silver bodies formed a glistening wake.

The prize residue was about five pounds of shrimps. Joe shot a dark stream of spit over the side, mumbling, "I never seen so few shrimp in my entire life. I think they all went over to Texas to get rich on the oil. Man, let's get outta here. I gotta go back to bricklayin' an' earn me some money before my wife begins complainin'. I sure hope trappin' ain't like this in the fall."

Other boats were heading back to Boston Canal, their crews wearing somber, hurt expressions. Not even bothering, this time, to cup their hands as they passed the docks along the canal, they just shook their heads while the waiting women nodded. Clifford, Randall, and Wyndal Stelly were in their little shed, slumped against the benches. There was no point in continuing to trawl.

"Hey, don't look so down," Joe yelled as he glided up to the dock. "Them shrimp just taking a little vacation. They'll be back in a few days, jus' you wait an' see. They know we're the bosses an' we expect 'em to get into the trawls. That's their job, an' if they don' cooperate, they're gonna get themselves fired."

The Stelly men responded with laughs only strong enough to let Joe know they accepted *him,* not the situation. They looked down at their feet uncertainly. The marsh had let them down, and its victims were dazed.

"Well, we got us plenty of crab, anyway," said Randall with a snorted half-chuckle.

"Yeah, ah sure hope ma rice come in good this year." Clifford ran his hand through his short white hair, as though meaning to put some order into it. "I dunno know, though." He shifted his weight from one leg to the other, supporting himself with a thick arm against one thigh. "It makes you think that somethin' gone funny somewhere when there ain't no shrimps."

By now most of the boats had returned from the bay, and Boston Canal was blanketed in the hot silence of midday. The glare stifled every sound, and it seemed as though time had stopped. The little world alongside the muddy water was limp and lay as though in wait for a passing cloud. The marsh grass was the only thing to move. It flowed in great waves, the sun glinting off its crest, from the Stellys' cabin all the way to where the shores of Avery Island flung up their hazy green.